COMPLETE BOOK OF MAGIC & MAGIC TRICKS

Cheryl Evans, Rebecca Heddle and Ian Keable-Elliott

Designed by Jane Felstead and Susie McCaffrey

CONTENTS

Illustrated by Paul Sullivan, Kim Blundell, Kim Raymond, John Davey, Chris Lyon, Ian Thompson and Joseph McEwan

ABOUT MAGIC

Magic is doing things that other people "know" are impossible. The art of the magician is to make it seem effortless and natural. People should be able to believe, if only for a short time, that you really have extraordinary powers.

The magicians in this picture are performing some of the different kinds of magic you will learn to do in this book.

Mentalism

Children's magic

Why do people like magic?

Despite the effects technology can achieve today, traditional magic is still very popular. Seeing an ordinary person do amazing things without the help of technology may be part of the appeal.

Magic is also a challenge. People are sure that if they concentrate hard enough they will be able to see how it is done.

Magicians are often funny and people enjoy laughing and being amazed at the same time. No matter what gets "lost" or "broken" during the act, it is all right in the end.

Magic is universal. Much magic does not require talking and can be appreciated worldwide.

How hard is it to learn?

You don't have to buy expensive equipment or be especially clever with your hands to do magic. There are tricks in this book that you will be able to do right away.

Others, though, do require special magic skills which are carefully explained and which you will need to learn and practice thoroughly. Gradually becoming more adept is part of the pleasure of doing magic.

Getting more from magic

If you are interested in magic, learning how to do it does not spoil the fun. Once you know some of its secrets you will understand the skill of experienced magicians and appreciate them even more.

Cabaret magic

Close-up magic

What is in this book

The first 25 pages of this book tell you about different kinds of magic and introduce some of the terms and skills you need to know to perform tricks well. There are also practical examples for you to try.

Starting on page 30, there are masses of tricks of all kinds explained in detail, step-by-step. As far as possible, the tricks are shown as if you are looking at your own hands so the moves are easy to follow. Where it helps, what the audience should see is shown as well.

On pages 26-29 you can read about the history of magic and some of the most famous magicians.

A good way to use this book is to read some of the presentation techniques in the first half. Then turn to the tricks section and try to apply what you have learned to a specific trick. As you learn more tricks, keep referring back to the tips and hints on making them interesting and original.

Learning more

This book provides you with the first steps to becoming a magician. You will become better by reading other books (you will find some suggestions on page 126) and by watching and meeting other magicians. Above all, you should start performing, as you will learn more from practical experience than any book or magician can teach you.

Keeping the secret

Magicians have a sort of code of honor which means that they do not tell magic secrets to outsiders. This book is for people who really want to perform magic so don't tell anyone who is not a good magician how you do the tricks.

KINDS OF MAGIC

The type of tricks you want to do, where you perform and the kind of audience you perform to all determine what kind of magic you do. You may enjoy showing a few simple tricks to your family and friends or want to be a professional with a glittering stage show. Most magic falls into one of the categories shown here.

Children's magic

A magician may perform for young children at a party in their home, or in schools as well as in theatres. They usually use colorful equipment which appeals to children. Some may dress up, too. Young children love to join in, so the magician must enjoy working with them.

Magic for fun

Many people learn a few magic tricks just for their own fun. There are lots you can do without buying equipment, using household things such as playing cards, coins or matches. You can even carry these in your pockets and do tricks on the spot. There is one to try on the next page.

Close-up magic

Close-up magicians perform for a small audience, using things they carry in their pockets or a small case. You can easily do this sort of magic at home. Professionals may perform in restaurants, doing the same short act for different tables. They often chat and joke with the audience.

Silent magic

Magic is rarely done in total silence as most silent artistes work to music. The way they look is especially important, so they take great care over their costumes, equipment, gestures and expressions. The best silent acts are the most skilled of all magicians.

Cabaret magic

Cabaret, or stand-up, magic is the kind you most often see on stage or television. A cabaret is a theatre where people sit at tables to eat and watch a show afterwards. The acts are often funny, and some use elaborate equipment or have an assistant to add variety.

Illusions

Illusions are "impossible" feats with living things, such as making an elephant disappear. This usually requires large and expensive equipment so performers need to be quite well-established before they can afford to do them. They often have the help of assistants.

Escapology

Escapology involves escaping from all kinds of bonds and prisons. The performer must be fit and agile and have lots of nerve, as some escapes are really dangerous. It helps to be able to pick locks and untie knots but there are trick techniques that can help.

Mentalism

A mentalist does tricks that seem to be superhuman feats of the mind. They vary from predicting the future and reading people's minds to bending metal forks. The audience must believe that the mentalists' powers are real so their looks must be convincing.

Where's the Coin?

Try this trick at a table. All you need is a coin. Practice on your own first to make sure you can do it expertly. Unlike most tricks, this one can be repeated several times.

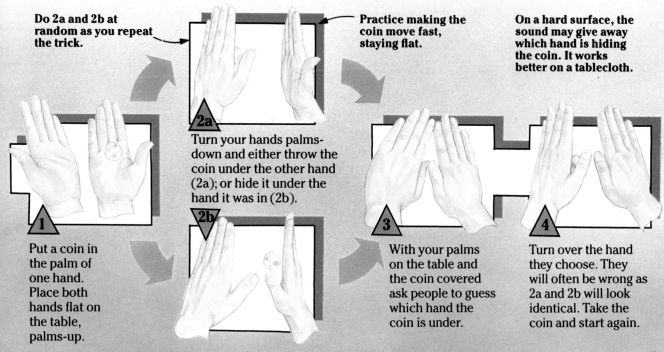

Do 2a and 2b at random as you repeat the trick.

Practice making the coin move fast, staying flat.

On a hard surface, the sound may give away which hand is hiding the coin. It works better on a tablecloth.

1 Put a coin in the palm of one hand. Place both hands flat on the table, palms-up.

2a / **2b** Turn your hands palms-down and either throw the coin under the other hand (2a); or hide it under the hand it was in (2b).

3 With your palms on the table and the coin covered ask people to guess which hand the coin is under.

4 Turn over the hand they choose. They will often be wrong as 2a and 2b will look identical. Take the coin and start again.

PROPS

Whatever kind of magic you do, you need props (short for properties). Anything used during a performance is called a prop. You can find out about different types of props below, plus some tips for actually using them.

Types of props

Props vary from everyday things, such as a handkerchief, to specially bought or made equipment. You may use a prop simply to show your magic powers, by making it disappear, for example. Or the prop itself may make the magic work, such as a box with a false bottom. Props are also useful for attracting the audience's attention from secret moves.

Rope

Egg Bag

Linking Rings

Fan

Cups and Balls

Dice

Cards

Top hat

Turban

Sword and Basket illusion

Silk scarves

"Thumb tips"

Flowers in pot

Servante

Wand

Children's prop

Fake boxes

Classic props

These are props that have been around for many years, but can be used in lots of fresh ways. The Linking Rings are one example. They link and come apart as the magician wishes.

Tricks for young children

These props are often brightly painted and feature themes that appeal to young children.

Traditional props

A top hat and wand are strongly linked with magic. Seeing them instantly tells people you are a magician.

Fakes and gimmicks

Fakes are familiar things that have been secretly altered. Gimmicks are props that are not seen, such as the servante in the picture.

Illusions

These are specially made props used by illusionists. They are expensive because you pay for the secret of how they work as much as for the equipment.

Live animals

Although you may occasionally see animals used in tricks, this can cause them accidental suffering as well as offending audiences. Don't imitate.

Tips on props

- *Mix special magic props with everyday things. People are often more amazed by magic done with familiar things than by strange gear.*

- *Be imaginative. Instead of a ball, use a small apple and hand it to someone after the trick. Or use a theme, such as Chinese props.*

- *Don't use too many props. If you can use the same one in several tricks, do so.*

- *Use appropriate props. A brightly colored box that is right for a children's act may not work in mentalism.*

- *Keep props in good condition. Wash and press silk scarves and re-paint boxes.*

- *Think about colors; blue props will not show against a blue shirt; lots of clashing colors look garish, for example.*

Magic Coin Spin

If you have a new, shiny coin, just spinning it as shown below will grab people's attention. This sort of eye-catching effect with a prop is called a flourish. Try it for yourself and when you can do it well, try the Magic Spin.

The flourish

Balance a coin on its rim on a table, with a flat side facing you. Rest your right first finger lightly on it to keep it upright. Flip your left first finger off your thumb to hit the flat face and make the coin spin. Lift your right finger as it starts.

The Magic Spin

Balance the coin as before. Stroke your left first finger along your right first finger a few times as if generating magic power. Have your left fingers curled, but stick your left thumb out underneath the finger balancing the coin.

Buying props

You can buy props in magic shops, some toy departments, and direct from magic dealers. In shops, assistants will often show you how they work. They vary a lot in price but need not be very expensive. You can even make some yourself (see pages 58-59).

(see pages 58-59).

Now stroke the left finger right off the end of the right, secretly flipping the coin with your left thumb to make it spin.

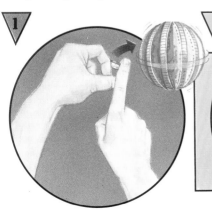

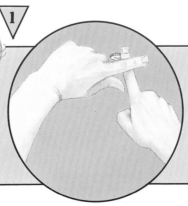

The audience does not see the flip. You seem to make the coin spin just by stroking.

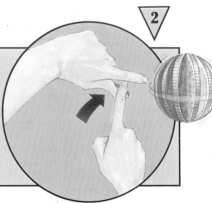

ACTING AND THE MAGICIAN

To be a good magician you do not have to pretend to be someone else, so don't worry if you think you cannot act. You do, however, need to think about how you look, speak and move during a performance. These are acting skills which you can find out about below.

Where you perform

The amount of acting you do can depend on where you perform. It may be appropriate to act an exaggerated character on a stage, but would seem silly for your friends and family at home. You also need to consider how many people are watching and how easily they can see.

On stage, playing a character can help entertain a large audience.

In close-up, a more natural style works better.

Acting tips

- Try to relax and stand naturally. Don't shuffle or fidget.

- Your hands especially may be a problem. When not holding props, let them hang casually at your sides or hold them at waist level, with elbows bent.

- React to your tricks. Look surprised, pleased and so on. If you seem indifferent, the audience will be, too.

- Your body is expressive, too. You can raise your shoulders in exasperation or scratch your head in puzzlement.

- Prepare what you are going to say and speak clearly. Don't speak too fast. You can read more on this subject on pages 12-13.

- Watch magicians and other performers on television to see what they do and pick up hints.

Slight of hand

Slight of hand is a name for secret moves in magic. Slights are necessary to make some tricks work and acting skills are vital to their success. This is a very useful slight, called the French Drop. You can also use it in the trick on the next page. Here it is shown from the audience's point of view.

Take a coin between your right thumb and first finger. Make sure everyone sees it.

Put your left hand over the coin as if to take it. Really, drop it onto your right fingers.

Your left hand hides what is happening.

Stagecraft

To make people feel part of the show, look directly at individuals as you talk to them.

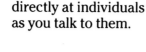 **Don't turn your back on people.** They soon get bored if they cannot see your face or hear you speak. To move backwards, cross the stage diagonally or simply step back.

Walk behind things ► you want seen, such as a prop or assistant. You can walk in front if what you are saying or doing is more important than anything else.

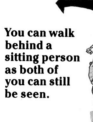

You can walk behind a sitting person as both of you can still be seen.

With these two silk hankies . . .

◄ It is hard for the audience to watch your face, listen and see what you are doing all at once. Try to avoid this unless you want to misdirect (see pages 10-11).

A name to conjure with

If you like, you can use a different name when you do magic. Some magicians like to invent one to suit their act: a funny one or a mock title such as "Professor" or a mysterious foreign name, for example.

Creating a character

Acting helps create a stage "persona". This is a character you may become when performing. A well-chosen and developed persona can improve your performance. It usually evolves over years of experience; don't try to force one on yourself.

This is the English magician, Tommy Cooper. He was a good magician, but seeming incompetent was part of his persona.

Close your left hand and move it away as if it has the coin. Follow it with your eyes.

Turn your left hand over, watching it with interest Let the right hand drop naturally.

Uncurl your left hand. Act amazed that the coin has gone and the audience will be, too.

Later, when the trick is over, put your right hand in your pocket and leave the coin there.

3 **Keep your right hand still.**

4

5

6

MISDIRECTION

Misdirection is a subtle skill used to hide secret moves. It takes thought and practice. The Coin Vanish trick at the bottom of the page uses the French Drop slight from the last page and some subtle misdirection.

Ways to misdirect

It may seem hard to hide things from an audience that is watching closely. In fact, it is quite easy to deceive them. Some ways are given here. Several may apply at once and work together to misdirect.

Eye foolers

People's eyes tell them things that may not be true. If you seem to swap a coin from one hand to the other convincingly, they believe what they think they have seen.

Attracting attention

If you draw attention to a prop in one hand, something hidden in the other will go unnoticed.

Allaying suspicions

Audiences are suspicious. They try to spot how tricks are done. To combat this, handle props casually and openly so there does not seem to be anything to hide. Let the audience examine some of them.

Using repetition

If you do the same thing again and again, the audience stops watching closely. You could shuffle cards in the same way several times before doing a slight with the same shuffle.

Where to look

Look directly at the audience and they will tend to look at your face; look at a prop or your hand, and they look at those.

The psychological moment

There are times when an audience is less alert, such as when a trick is just over. They don't expect more magic yet. If you do a slight then, it is less likely to be seen.

Big versus small

A big noise or gesture hides a smaller one. Plan to make a deliberate loud noise part of your act to hide a slight that makes a little noise, such as a coin clinking.

Time lapse

Memories are short, especially if lots is going on. If you are left with a prop hidden in your hand, wait a bit so people forget. Then get rid of it.

Coin Vanish

Place a coin and wand (or use a pencil) on a table. Take the coin in your right hand and show it to the audience.

Look at the wand as if you want to pick it up but cannot because of the coin. This creates a reason to do the next step.

Pretend to swap the coin to your left hand, but really French Drop it into your right. Keep looking at the wand.

1

People look where you look, not at your hands.

2

3

10

Tips on misdirection

- *Don't rely on slights being perfect; use misdirection as well, to be sure.*

- *Always invent a good reason for doing something. If you want to take something secretly from your pocket, do it when you are openly putting something away.*

- *Match your misdirection to your style. If your act is low key, a sudden shout or gesture would seem out of place. A wry joke or amusing expression might be more suitable.*

Misdirection or distraction?

You can easily distract people for a moment by exclaiming and pointing at the ceiling. This is not misdirection. The audience would know it had been tricked and would not be fooled more than once or twice.

Misdirection in close-up

You may think that misdirection is trickier when the audience is close to you. In fact, it is hard for them to focus on more than a small part of you at once. Here's how you can make use of this:

Find out people's names and use them. They will look up at your face and away from your hands.

Ask people to help, by shuffling cards, perhaps. Other spectators will watch them, diverting attention from you.

From this close, the spectator cannot watch your face and hands at the same time.

Misdirection on stage

When you are on stage, people can see everything you do at a glance. You may need to use bigger gestures to misdirect. Here are some other techniques that help:

Spectator can take all of you in at the same time.

Using volunteers from the audience or having an assistant on stage takes attention away from you.

What you say misdirects. You can lead the audience to expect one thing, so they are surprised when something else happens.

Pick up the wand with your right hand, too. Now turn your attention to your left fist, where the coin is meant to be.

Tap your left fist with the wand as if working magic. (Really, the magic was in step 3. This time delay helps to misdirect.)

Uncurl your hand slowly, watching with interest. React with surprise or delight that the coin has gone.

Audience responds to your reaction.

PATTER

Patter is the name for what you say during an act. It should sound natural but, in fact, a lot of work goes into making it informative and amusing.

What to say

Build a framework of patter around things you must say, such as introducing yourself, greeting the audience, explaining what they need to know and linking tricks.

Pitfalls to avoid

Here are some examples of things not to say:

Stating the obvious

> I am now picking up this handkerchief.

The audience can see what you are doing. You don't need to say it as well.

Arousing suspicions

> I put it in this envelope, which is quite standard and has not been tampered with in any way.

You would not expect there to be anything odd about an envelope. Stating it may put ideas into people's heads.

Spoiling the surprise

> And when I pull it out again it will have turned green.

As a general rule, avoid anticipating the effect by what you say.

Making it more interesting

As you get more confident, you can expand and improve your patter with some of the following ideas:

Storytelling

You could tell the history of a ▶ trick if it has an interesting origin. Or make up a story in which the magic becomes part of the action. Be careful not to make the story too long or the audience may get bored.

This rope trick is said to be a very old Indian effect.

Fantasy

◀ Particularly for acts or tricks involving mentalism or mind-reading, you can suggest that the tricks are done by the power of the mind or with the assistance of unknown forces.

Humour

It is quite hard to be funny, ▶ but here are some tips:

Make jokes relevant. A gag that is unrelated to the trick is simply distracting.

Keep it short. What comedians call "one-liners" work well. These are short, funny asides dropped into your speech.

Work on your timing. This means choosing the moment to tell a joke, pausing before the punchline for impact and allowing time for laughter afterwards. You can only learn timing by experience.

> I keep going to pieces today.

Tips on talking

- *In close-up magic use your normal voice. On a stage you may need to talk more slowly and clearly than usual. If there is a microphone (see below), speak normally.*

- *Talk naturally. Don't worry about your accent. It can be part of your persona (see page 9). As long as you talk clearly, people will understand.*

- *Cut out annoying speech habits, such as "you know" and "sort of" and using clichés. If you don't think you do any of these, ask a friend to listen to you and criticize.*

- *Use patter to create drama. Talk gradually more slowly to show concentration and build up suspense, for instance. Talk louder and faster at the climax.*

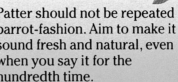

Patter should not be repeated parrot-fashion. Aim to make it sound fresh and natural, even when you say it for the hundredth time.

Using microphones

There is no need to shout.

A microphone amplifies your voice so it can be heard by everyone. You talk quite normally. The most important thing for performers is that their hands are free to handle props while they are speaking. Nowadays, clip-on microphones can be attached to a lapel or hung around your neck.

Rehearsed patter

You may find it quite hard at first to manipulate props and talk at the same time, so be sure to rehearse both together.

Ad-libs

Ad-libs are unrehearsed comments that occur to you. They can put you off your stride if you are not careful. If you like you can prepare "ad-lib" lines and use them if the chance arises. These are not true ad-libs but still work if they seem spontaneous.

Patter to avoid

Insulting the audience. Some professional magicians get away with this, but you cannot expect to.

Jokes about people's race or sex or issues they may feel deeply about such as religion or politics.

Too many puns, except for children, as they love bad puns.

Illogical patter, such as a very young magician referring to "my wife".

"Dirty" or "blue" jokes.

Other people's patter. Someone else's lines will not sound so good when you say them and audiences will not be impressed by your lack of originality.

Looking for patter

Here are some places to look for ideas for patter:

Books about magic for the history of tricks. (There are some suggested titles on page 62.)

Look out for odd stories in the newspapers.

Joke books, comics, television or funny things your friends say.

Keep a notebook of things you want to remember.

SILENT ACTS

Not all magicians use patter. Some illusionists perform silently to dramatic music, for instance. To magicians, a silent act usually means one performed to music, involving tricks using more manipulation skills than in a patter act. Below you can see some of the ways a silent act differs from a patter act.

You cannot get your personality across by words, so you must be interesting to look at. Costume and gestures show your persona.

You have to do more magic as there are no jokes or stories to help entertain. Magic must happen continuously.

Your slight of hand must be excellent and your misdirection convincing, as you have no other means to divert attention.

You can less afford to make mistakes as it is harder to bluff your way out. You must rehearse even more than other magicians.

Silent artistes sometimes use other skills such as mime or dance to help entertain during their act.

All aspects of the show must be as perfect as possible. People notice clothes, music and props more if there is no patter to listen to.

The act may be quite short since it demands a lot of audience concentration, which can only be maintained for short periods.

A good silent act is probably the hardest to do well but, if you succeed, it can be performed anywhere in the world.

Choosing and using music

Use a variety of music, making sure the different pieces flow smoothly from one to the next. As a guide, use cheerful music for your entrance, gentle tunes to relax the audience and something exciting for a climax. Don't choose a recent hit record or it will soon seem dated. Record your choices on a cassette and always rehearse to it. It is crucial to tie music and tricks together. A certain sequence of tricks must coincide exactly with a specific piece of music.

COSTUME

You don't have to have special clothes to do magic. You can perform in casual gear, but most people performing for an audience feel they want to dress the part. What you wear depends on the show you do and impression you want to make.

What to wear

A good general rule is to wear something smarter than your audience. As most magic is performed at a special night out or party, the kind of clothes these magicians have on should be suitable.

Labels round the picture show some important points about clothes for magicians. You might wear something very different for street performing, say, or to create a persona.

Jacket has plenty of pockets, inside and outside, which a magician can use.

Smart trousers also have back and side pockets.

Make sure shoes are clean and socks match. People will focus on anything odd or scruffy.

Silk scarf in hair can be taken out and used in tricks.

Secret pockets can be hidden in folds and belts.

Jewellery, fake flowers and so on can be used as props.

A bag is a good place to carry props.

Other styles

Some magicians wear a bright or glittery costume. These are specially made and cost a lot.

A traditional black tailcoat is elegant and versatile. Hat, gloves and wand are useful accessories.

Character costumes may be worn in a pantomime or play. This magician is dressed as a wizard.

Doctored costumes

Some people think magicians have lots of secret pockets and other hiding places. In fact, they mostly use existing pockets and natural hiding places in a lapel or belt. Special devices are sometimes used, though:

This is a bag holder. It opens at the bottom to let a prop drop into your hand.

This small pocket on the outside of a costume is a dip pocket. It is in matching cloth, at arm's length.

A pocket inside a jacket or under a coat tail, like this, is a toppit.

Where to get costumes

Rent them from a theatrical costumier or fancy dress shop. Find them in your phone book.

Evening wear rent shops often have sales of used stock.

Search in junk shops for second-hand evening clothes, accessories and props.

If you are good at sewing you could make your own.

REHEARSING

Before you do a trick you must rehearse it thoroughly. It takes a lot of practice to get the movements perfect and think of an interesting presentation. Read about ways to rehearse below then try them out on the trick at the bottom of the page.

Practicing slights

Follow the pink arrow and instructions to rehearse this Finger Palm slight.

Practice in a mirror to make sure it looks natural. Once you feel confident, stop using the mirror and try not to look at your hands. Most slights can be used in many tricks.

The pictures in circles show what you see in the mirror.

In the mirror, the real move and slight should look the same.

Move this hand away.

Slight.

Start here. The moves are shown from your own point of view.

Keep this hand still.

Practice the real move first, then do the slight to look the same.

Real move.

⭐**1**

Hold up the coin between the thumb and first two fingers of your right hand. Do it quite casually.

⭐**2**

Bring your left hand over your right so its fingers hide the coin. Don't hesitate, but carry smoothly on to the next step.

⭐**3**

First, take the coin and move your left hand away. For the slight, pretend to do the same, but actually drop the coin onto your right fingers.

Coin Through a Handkerchief

To rehearse this trick, practice the slight on its own first, as shown above. Then work on the other aspects involved in making a trick successful, such as patter, misdirecting the audience and linking the trick to those that come before and after. To do it you need a coin and a handkerchief.

Bump

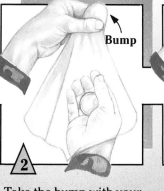

🔺**1**

Hold up the coin in your right hand. With your left hand, drape a handkerchief over it. There is a bump where the coin is.

🔺**2**

Take the bump with your left hand. People think this is the coin. In fact, use the slight above to drop the coin into your right fingers.

🔺**3**

Lift the handkerchief off your right hand, still gripping the bump. You leave the coin in your right hand.

How to rehearse a trick

Here are some steps to take when thinking about how to perform a trick. The magician on the right points out how to apply some of them to the trick at the bottom of the page.

Work on individual slights.

Familiarize yourself with the props and make sure they work.

Try to spot weak points, when people may see how the trick is done. Decide how to misdirect.

Work out what to say from start to finish.

Work out how you will link tricks.

Perform the trick right through several times.

You need a handkerchief that will keep the shape of the coin even when it is not really there. Crisp linen is better than silk.

Step 5 is a danger spot. Talk, so people don't look at your hands.

A good link would be to do the trick on page 19 next.

Rehearsal tips

- *You can always improve a trick. Keep working on it.*
- *Wear the clothes you will wear on stage.*
- *Perfect a small number of tricks rather than do a lot sloppily.*
- *Treat the first time you do a new trick as another rehearsal. You cannot know if it works until you perform for real.*
- *Rehearse frequently but in small doses. You are more likely to overcome a problem when you come to it fresh.*
- *Try a new trick on friends or family and listen to their criticisms. If you have access to a video, film yourself and criticize your performance.*

Stage fright

Stage fright is an attack of nerves on stage. You forget what you are saying and make mistakes. Thorough rehearsal reduces the risk of it. Being scared before you start is anticipation not stage fright.

Coin under handkerchief.

4 Lay the handkerchief on your right palm, on top of the coin that is hidden there. The audience still thinks the bump is where the coin is.

Have hands parallel to floor while you do this.

5 Pass your left hand back towards you close underneath your right hand, taking the coin from your right hand with your left.

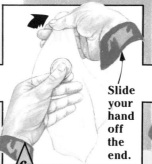

6 Grip the handkerchief with your left hand. Pretend to try and squeeze the coin out through the end of it with your right hand.

Slide your hand off the end.

Coin appears here.

7 Under the handkerchief, take the coin from your left hand with your right fingers. Let it emerge from the bump as if through the material.

ASSISTANTS, VOLUNTEERS AND STOOGES

Many magicians use helpers. They may be trained assistants who always rehearse and work with them. Or they can be volunteers from the audience. The trick on the page opposite depends on another kind of helper called a stooge that you can find out about below. You will need to teach a friend to do it with you.

Assistants

Some assistants are unobtrusive. They hand things to the performer and quietly remove props that are finished with, for example. They dress discreetly and are hardly noticed by the audience.

Others play a more active role. They may display props, take part in tricks, provide misdirection or even pretend to be clumsy or incompetent for a funny effect.

Stooges

A stooge is someone from the audience posing as a volunteer. The magician tells him before the show what to do and say to make the trick work. It can be a problem for the helper to act naturally so no-one else suspects he is a stooge.

Some professionals can make genuine volunteers act as stooges by telling them secretly what to do once up on stage. Most people will be prepared to go along with it, but it is risky.

Volunteers and how to choose them

Volunteers are picked from the audience to watch or to help. It is quite often hard to see and judge spectators to choose a good volunteer. If possible (for instance in close-up magic), chat to the audience before the show.

If the lighting makes seeing difficult, walk out among the audience for a better look.

Volunteers should seem to be chosen randomly, but here are some things to look out for to find good ones:

A person whose looks contrast with yours.

People obviously having fun.

Reactions that might add to the effect, such as giggles.

Someone to reinforce an impression: a big man to test the strength of a prop, say.

Someone from a large group; their family or friends will egg them on.

For real randomness, throw something easy to catch, such as a ping-pong ball, and ask whoever catches it.

Tips on volunteers

- *People who choose to sit near the front are usually quite keen to volunteer.*

- *Make sure they will have no physical difficulty helping.*

- *Treat them well, thank them and ask for applause. See them safely back off stage.*

- *Give clear instructions.*

- *Use them in the middle of an act. They can be distracting during your first trick or when taking your final bow.*

- *Don't use them for the sake of it. What they do must enhance the act.*

Coin Vanish with Handkerchief

This trick is a version of the trick on pages 16-17. To perform it, you need a stooge. He or she must keep a straight face and not give anything away. Rehearse together thoroughly. In these pictures you see what the audience sees.

1 Hold the coin up and show it to the audience. Then cover it with a handkerchief, as in the previous trick.

2 Take hold of the coin and the handkerchief with your left hand, and lift them both off your right hand.

3 Ask a spectator to feel the coin. Insist his hand goes under the handkerchief. Repeat with other spectators.

Spectator

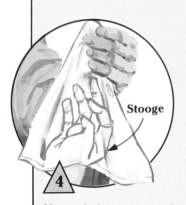

Stooge

4 Now ask the stooge and let him take the coin when he withdraws his hand. If he can Finger Palm it, he should.

5 Go through steps 4 and 5 of the trick on page 17, ignoring the coin because you no longer have it. This is good time misdirection; it separates the moment when the trick took place (when the stooge took the coin) from the revelation that the coin has gone. People forget who last touched the coin under the handkerchief and do not think it is important, anyway.

6 This step is the same as step 6 on page 17 only, as you stroke, look puzzled that the coin does not appear.

7 Finally, give up and shake out the handkerchief to show that the coin has completely vanished.

Advantages of using helpers

Many tricks cannot be performed without help, so using assistants and volunteers increases the range of tricks you can do.

Using volunteers involves the audience so the act is more interesting to them.

An enthusiastic assistant will give help and support and may be able to make useful suggestions for improving the act

Jokes and chat with helpers provide variety and help fill out the act.

Disadvantages of using helpers

Assistants work as hard as magicians, without much credit. They may get fed up and leave to follow their own career.

Getting people to volunteer can be difficult and may embarrass the audience.

Volunteers can spoil a trick, accidentally or even on purpose.

Working professionally, it is hard to get twice as much money as on your own, but you must still pay your helper.

WHEN THINGS GO WRONG

Every "live" performer dreads something going wrong and, in magic, the risk is quite high. Thorough rehearsal should prevent most mistakes but unforeseen problems will still arise. The information on these two pages will help you avoid or deal with tricky situations, but only experience can really make you confident.

About your audience

At first, it is easy to feel that the audience is just waiting for you to do something wrong. In fact, people are not nearly as critical as you think and are really on your side. Try to remember these points:

People would rather be entertained than simply fooled. As long as they enjoy the show they will not worry if they see how a trick is done or detect a slight.

Most people realize and respect how hard magic is. If a trick fails, they feel sympathy. Don't embarrass them by getting flustered and over-apologizing, and they will probably warm to you all the more.

People have very short memories. They are more likely to remember your successful tricks than mistakes.

You are very conscious of mistakes, but an audience may not even notice them.

Avoiding problems with props

Make a check list of where your props should be at the start of the act. Use it each time you set up. Always check that props work just before you perform, even if they worked fine the last time you used them.

Avoiding problems with people

It is up to you to ensure that volunteers do what you want them to.

Avoid asking questions if the wrong answer could spoil your trick.

If a volunteer ruins a trick abandon it and get him politely off stage.

Tips on coping

Here are some ideas that could prevent disaster when you make a mistake:

- *You may be able to change the ending by doing a different magic effect. The audience doesn't know what you had planned, so they will not even notice.*

- *Start again, if your mistake has not revealed any secrets. Tell the audience what you are doing. They will think the trick must be difficult and be all the more impressed when you succeed.*

- *If all else fails, move on to a new trick. Joke about it if you can. If you are not uneasy, others will not be.*

More serious problems

If your whole act goes down badly, it may be for one of the reasons below. There are suggestions to help solve the problems, too.

Problem: You genuinely do not perform the act well on one particular evening.

Solution: Try to develop a routine to help key yourself up and prepare for each performance.

Problem: The audience is not in a receptive mood. This may be because they have other distractions, such as food (in a restaurant) or dancing and chatting (at a party).

Solution: All you can do is perform to the best of your ability and hope to catch one or two people's attention. Once a few people start to watch, others usually follow through curiosity.

Problem: The act may not be suitable for that particular audience.

Solution: Try to find out what sort of audience to expect where you are performing. The same act can be made to suit different audiences by a subtle change of patter or presentation.

"Dying" on stage

When a whole act is badly received it is called "dying". If the audience is clearly not watching or starts to make critical comments, you know something is seriously wrong. It is better to struggle on rather than stopping, for these reasons:

You may do a trick later which people like so you win back their attention.

You will find out far more about your act, and what is wrong with it, by performing to the end.

People like performers who don't give in. You may gain their respect, at least, if you keep trying.

Coin Recovery

Here you can see how a mistake can be made into part of the act. If you accidentally drop a coin while doing the French Drop, say, you could pick it up and try again but the audience may have seen it fall from the "wrong" hand and realize how the slight is done. Instead, try this trick.

Place one foot near the coin on the floor. If you need to get nearer to it, move around as though looking for it.

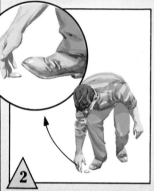

2 Bend down to pick up the coin but, actually, lift your toe and slide the coin under it as you close your hand.

3 Stand up and say you will try again. Pretend to put the coin into the other hand.

4 With a magic gesture, open the hand that is meant to have the coin in it, then the other. The coin has vanished.

5 If you have a spare coin you can now carry on as you originally intended. Or move on to another trick. Although this leaves you with your foot on the coin so you cannot move around, don't try to pick it up too soon. You could do another trick in which a coin vanishes and "appears" under your foot. Or deliberately let something else drop and pick up the coin at the same time.

PLANNING AN ACT

Magicians usually plan a linked series of tricks to form an act. You can build an act gradually from tricks that you like doing and perform well. Rather than just letting it grow haphazardly, though, it is a good idea to think honestly about your own strengths and weaknesses and the kind of audience you expect to perform for. You can then use the tips below to help work out a balanced performance.

Things to consider when planning an act

If you find it easy to chat to all kinds of people you will probably enjoy doing a patter act. You will get more personal contact in close-up work than a stage act.

If you are good at telling jokes and being funny, plan a comedy act. If not, don't force it. You might try to amaze the audience with your dexterity, elegance or dramatic effects instead.

Experiment with different styles to discover the one you enjoy most. If you enjoy yourself, the audience should, too.

If you want to do a silent act, you might feel you could benefit from mime or acting lessons.

Shaping an act

This curved orange path shows the ideal shape of an act. Read how to include pace and variety by starting at the Opening, below, and following the path to the Finish on the next page. The basic shape is the same whatever your act.

It is a golden rule of magic only to work with young children if you genuinely enjoy it.

On the notepads are tricks from this book which fit in the places shown.

Close-up:
Instant Revelation
Pegasus

Children's:
Hello Routine

Cabaret:
Cut and Restored Rope

Silent:
Miser's Dream

Upward curves show where exciting things happen.

Downward curves show quieter moments. They are necessary to provide contrast and give the audience a chance to relax.

The Opening

First impressions are vital so start with something short but exciting. Let the audience get to know you. Don't introduce an assistant or use a volunteer yet.

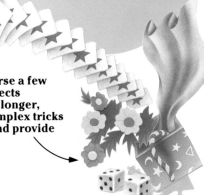

Intersperse a few short effects between longer, more complex tricks to link and provide variety.

The Middle

Do longer tricks here. If you have people's attention, they will not mind waiting a bit for a good climax. Use an assistant for variety. The audience should be relaxed now, so it is a good time to ask for volunteers, too.

Cabaret:
Glasses and Bottles

Escapology:
Sack Escape

Children's:
Toy Rabbit Production

Mentalism:
Newspaper Prediction

Close-up:
Do As I Do
Copper and Silver

Cabaret:
Coin in Wool
Two Card Trick

Children's:
Farmyard Noises

The general trend of the act is upwards. Quieter moments should not let interest drop back to the level before the previous peak.

The Finish

Save your most spectacular trick for last. Producing something is better than making it vanish as people can see and applaud it. Don't use helpers here, so you can take your final bow alone.

Lengths of acts

It is impossible to say how long an act should be as they vary so much. There are basic differences between the average lengths of different sorts of act, though, as this table shows.

Type of magic	Time in minutes	Comments
Close-up	5-10	You will probably be expected to repeat the act several times to different groups of people over a period of 1 to 3 hours.
Cabaret	20-45	To keep the audience entertained for this length of time, cabaret acts usually involve plenty of humour.
Silent	10	Silent acts tend to be shorter because magic is happening all the time, which requires a lot of concentration from the audience and magician.
Children's	30-60	Children need plenty of variety and excitement to hold their attention. Doing magic for children can be exhausting.
Illusions Mentalism Escapology	5-60	A full-length show in these styles might last an hour but a magician may also do just one trick in a variety show.

Audiences rarely complain that an act is too short. It's a good idea to leave them wanting more.

It is very hard to be a professional magician. The best preparation is to get as much performing experience as you can.

Many magicians start as semi-professionals, which means doing magic while still holding an ordinary job.

Getting started

It is worth doing any magic work so that people get to know you. Your reputation will spread mainly by word of mouth at first. You could get a card printed to give to anyone who shows an interest in you.

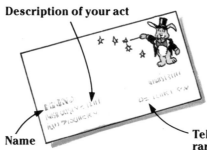

Description of your act

Name

Telephone number (people rarely write to book).

For wider publicity, ask a local paper to send a reporter to see you. Enclose a ticket and mention that you are a new, young magicians.

Opportunities to perform

Finding places to perform takes a lot of effort. There are more opportunities to perform some kinds of magic than others. Here are some suggestions:

Hospitals and homes

Offer to perform for your local hospital, children's or retirement home. They are unlikely to be able to pay, though you might get expenses. Try to contact someone in charge of entertainments.

Parties

Magicians can usually find plenty of work at children's parties and sometimes at adults' parties, too. People look for a magician in their area, so an advertisement in the local telephone directory or paper could be useful.

Charities

A local charity might help you organize a show and sell tickets if you perform to raise money for their funds. Call or write and suggest it.

Cruises

Some cruise operators book cabaret acts for an evening, one trip or a whole season.

Talent contests

Talent contests are held to find good new acts. You compete against other acts such as singers or comedians, and it is good experience. Contests are advertised in newspapers or locally. You may have to travel to your nearest big town to attend.

Hotels and restaurants

Close-up and cabaret work may be found in hotels and restaurants. See if the owner or manager is interested.

Magic for businesses

A company may employ a magician to promote products at trade shows or business parties. Try approaching a suitable firm's Public Relations officer.

Street performing

Vacation places often allow street entertaining. Check with the police whether you need permission.

Discos

Magic in discos is becoming popular. Your act must work against a background of disco music and lights.

Theatres and cabarets

For most theatre or cabaret work you need an agent (see next page). For experience, ask an amateur drama group if they could use you in a play.

Survival as a professional

◀ You must be prepared to work under almost any conditions. Don't restrict yourself to one style of act. Work for children and adults. You can specialize later as you find more of the kind of work you enjoy.

◀ To succeed, you need skills other than magic ones. You must be able to handle the business side, deal with potential bookers, behave agreeably off-stage and be as courteous as possible with everyone, even if they are not polite to you.

◀ Insist on professionalism. Try to get a contract for a booking, or at least a confirming letter. Make sure you and the booker both know what you expect – the style of show, size of audience, length of performance and so on.

◀ Always turn up on time and don't perform for longer than requested. Try to speak to people after the show. This is an opportunity to make contacts, hand out business cards and find more work.

◀ Nearly all magicians sometimes get fed up. You may have very little work or a show may go badly. Try to keep looking forward and working on your act and things should improve.

Asking for money

If you want to make a living from magic you must charge for it. The amount depends on the kind of act, the venue and your experience.

Find out what people with a similar act charge and ask the same. Don't take a much reduced fee as this undermines other professional magicians.

Agents

An agent is someone to whom people apply to book an act. If your name is on an agent's list, it will be put forward for suitable work.

You pay a percentage of your fee for this service. You can ask an agent to take you on but he will want to see your act and decide for himself.

Managers

A manager promotes you and goes out looking for work for you. He or she usually demands a high salary or percentage of your earnings. A manager will only offer to take you on if you have the potential to earn a lot.

THE STORY OF MAGIC

From ancient times

Magic has probably been used from the earliest times by witch doctors and other wonder workers.

In Ancient Greece and Rome, priests used magic to produce "miraculous" effects during religious ceremonies. Secret mechanisms could make temple doors open by themselves or wine flow from statues.

The earliest records

The oldest written record of a magic performance is in an Egyptian scroll dated about 2600 BC. It tells of an illusionist called Dedi entertaining the Pharaoh, Cheops.

In the first century AD, a Roman called Seneca wrote about seeing a magician. He described the cup and balls trick, in which balls appear and disappear under three upturned beakers. It is still widely performed today.

Dangerous times

In Medieval Europe, magic was confused with witchcraft, which was punishable by death. In 1584, an Englishman called Reginald Scot wrote a book called *The Discoverie of Witchcraft*. It showed how some slights were done to prove that it was not with the help of the Devil.

Travelling showmen

For a long time, magic was not respectable. In the 16th century, magicians travelled around performing where they could. They often set up booths at fairs and markets.

Novelties, such as stone-swallowing, were popular, as well as conventional magic. From the late 16th century, there were many "intelligent" animal acts. A man called Banks and his horse, Marocco, were a great success in London in the 1580s, for example.

Marocco counted by tapping his hoof and could identify people in the audience from a description of them.

Fashions in magic

In the early 19th century, "scientific" tricks were the rage because of public interest in new scientific discoveries. Some performers called themselves Doctor or Professor and gave a mock lecture before their act.

A French magician called Robert-Houdin (see next page) did a levitation illusion, claiming he used the newly-discovered gas, ether.

Great magic shows

At the end of the 19th and start of the 20th centuries spectacular magic shows travelled from theatre to theatre. One American illusionist, Howard Thurston, needed ten railway cars to transport all his equipment at one time.

Dante was born in Denmark. Sim Sala Bim were nonsense words from a Danish nursery rhyme.

Among the greatest of these showmen were Harry Blackstone Senior, Dante and his show called *Sim Sala Bim* and an Indian magician called P.C. Sorcar.

A home for magic

It was many magicians' dream to be able to stop travelling and perform in a permanent magic venue. Not many realized their dream.

One who did was John Nevil Maskelyne. With his partners, first George Cooke and later David Devant, he presented magic in the Egyptian Hall and later St. George's Hall in London for over 40 years from 1873.

Modern magic

In recent years, television has given magicians their largest audiences. The magic still thrills people, especially if they believe no camera tricks are used.

The future of magic

Advances in technology, such as holograms and lasers, may seem almost magical. Still, simple tricks done by a magician before your eyes are as baffling today as in ancient times. This is unlikely to change.

FAMOUS NAMES

Modern magic is usually said to have begun in the 19th century. Here are some of the most famous names in magic since that time.

Top hat and tails were common formal wear in the late 19th century.

The Father of modern magic

The French magician, Jean Eugène Robert-Houdin is often called the "Father of modern magic". He was an expert watchmaker and inventor who made gadgets for his home as well as magic props. He only took up magic full-time when he was over fifty. His original idea was to present himself as an ordinary man who just happened to be able to do extraordinary things.

The Wizard of the North

A Scotsman called John Henry Anderson was among the first to realize that success depended on good promotion. He made sure of large audiences by giving plenty of advance warning that he was coming to town and toured extensively in Britain and the United States in the 19th century. He sometimes billed himself by the catchy title The Wizard of the North.

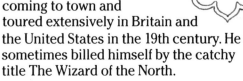

Individualists

As magic increased in popularity, entertainers had to do something different to get noticed.

◄ Chung Ling Soo was really William Ellsworth Robinson, an American imitating a Chinese magician. He kept up his Chinese persona at all times in public. He died on stage in 1918 attempting a trick in which he caught a bullet in his mouth. The gun was faulty and fired a real bullet that killed him.

Harry Houdini was ► born in 1874 in Hungary as Ehrich Weiss. He changed his name to Houdini as a tribute to Robert-Houdin. Possibly the greatest showman ever, his name became a household word through his daring feats of escapology.

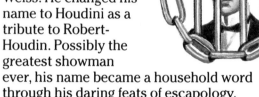

Two American brothers, Ira and William Davenport, exploited the rage for spiritualism (contacting the dead) in the 19th century. They were tied up and locked in a cabinet from which strange noises and objects then emerged. They claimed these were supernatural. Really they were escape artists who did the effects themselves.

▼

Inventors

Some magicians are famous more for inventing a very famous trick than for their own performances.

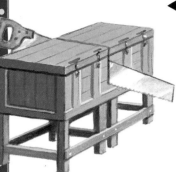

◀ In 1921, the British magician P.T. Selbit invented and performed for the first time the world's most famous trick, "Sawing Through a Woman".

Buatier de Kolta ▶ invented the "Vanishing Birdcage" in which a live canary disappeared with its cage. It caused an uproar over cruelty to the canary. In Britain a magician even did the trick for politicians to satisfy them that no harm came to the bird. Some say the trick was done differently in the test and the canary was lucky this time.

◀ The most famous inventor of recent times was Robert Harbin. He invented the "Zig-Zag Girl" trick, in which a girl's middle seems to be removed.

Kings of manipulation

T. Nelson Downs was called the King of Koins because of his spectacular silent act with coins. ▶

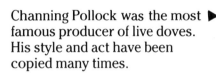

◀ Cardini seemed to produce dozens of fans of cards from nowhere. He learned his skills in World War I trenches, where it was so cold that he practiced in gloves. Later, white gloves and a monocle became his trademarks.

Channing Pollock was the most ▶ famous producer of live doves. His style and act have been copied many times.

Close-up

Not many close-up artists become widely known as they can only perform for a few people at once. Perhaps the most famous in this century were Max Malini and Nate Leipzig. Another great close-up performer, Canandian-born Dai Vernon, has recorded their lives and tricks.

Magicians on television

Television has made many magicians famous, including Fred Kaps from Holland, Britain's Paul Daniels and David Copperfield from the United States.

In the 1970s, a man called Uri Geller frequently entertained on television. He claimed to bend forks and make watches stop or start by the power of his mind. Magicians say they can duplicate all his effects.

CARDS: FIRST HANDLING SKILLS

Playing cards can be used in a wider variety of tricks than any other prop. On the next six pages you can learn to handle them expertly. The actual cards may vary but these skills apply to any pack.

When you try any trick in this part of the book, first read the steps and look at the pictures carefully. Remember that how to do it is only one side of the trick. You must think of good presentations, too.

About playing cards

Cards are cheap, colorful and easy to obtain, so they are ideal to start doing magic with.

Decks of cards come in different sizes. Use whichever suits you best.

The deck, or a card, is "face-down" when you can see the patterned back and "face-up" when you can see the value and suit.

Look for decks with a white border around the pattern on the back. This helps disguise various secret moves as it is the same color as the face of the card.

It is well worth mastering basic handling skills before trying to perform any tricks.

Overhand Shuffle

This simple but effective shuffle can be adapted to help in tricks (see the Shuffle Control on page 35).

Try to develop a rhythm.

Long edge

Short edge

Practise until you can shuffle without looking.

Try drawing off one card at a time.

1 Rest the deck on a long edge in your left hand. Hold the short edges with your right fingers and thumb.

2 Press on the deck with your left thumb. Lift your right hand and draw some cards into your left.

3 Lift the deck over the drawn-off cards and repeat 2 and 3 until all the cards are in your left hand.

Squaring the deck

After shuffling, you may need to tidy, or square, the deck. Tap the edges on a table to make them even or use your hands like this:

The Three Burglars

This is a self-working trick, which means that it doesn't need any slight of hand, but you should still work on the presentation. To prepare, put a red ace on top of the face-down deck and a three on the bottom. You can do this by looking through the cards, face-up, and cutting them into place. Chat while you do it, then put the cards down for a moment before going on so people forget what you were up to.

Openly search the deck and take out the other threes and red ace. Put them on a table, face-down, with the ace on the bottom. Place the deck by them.

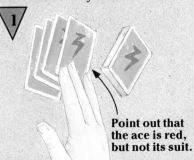

1

Point out that the ace is red, but not its suit.

Tell the audience that the deck is a house and the threes are burglars. Show them a three then put it on top of the deck, saying this burglar got in by the roof.

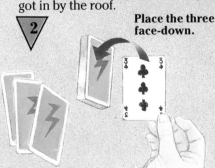

2

Place the three face-down.

Cutting the cards

Cutting means dividing the deck in two and putting the half that was on the bottom on the top. However many times you cut the deck, the order of the cards does not change. You can cut the cards on a table. The Kick Cut, below, is a neat way to do it in your hands.

Kick Cut

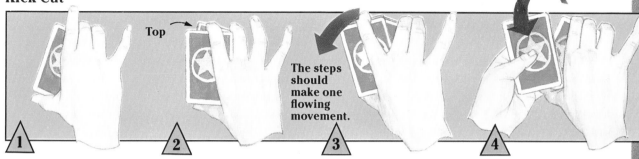

Top

The steps should make one flowing movement.

1 Hold the deck face-down by its short edges with your right fingers and thumb.

2 With your right first finger, lift about half the cards off the deck at the top short edge.

3 Swivel the lifted cards to the left, pivoting on your thumb, ready to take in your left hand.

4 Take them with your left hand, then put the cards that are in your right hand on top.

Classic Card Spread

Many card tricks involve a spectator picking a card. The magician often spreads the cards to let him choose. This is how to do a Classic Spread. Do it in a straight line or make a slight fan-shape. Note that the cards are in the same order when you close them together again.

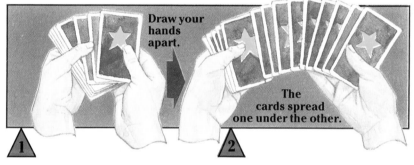

Draw your hands apart.

The cards spread one under the other.

1 Hold the deck flat in your left hand. With your left thumb, push cards off the top of the deck into your right hand a few at a time.

2 Spread the cards into a rough line or fan. Support them with your fingers underneath and your thumbs on top.

Say the next burglar got in by the cellar (put a three under the deck). The third climbed in a top floor window (put this card in a third down the deck).

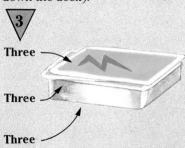

3

Three
Three
Three

Pick up the ace and say it is a policeman who enters the ground floor (put it in two thirds down the deck). Cut the pack a few times, saying there is a chase.

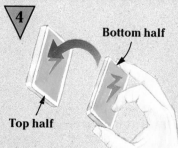

4

Bottom half

Top half

Spread the cards face-up. A red ace and three threes will appear together somewhere in the deck so you can say that the policeman caught the burglars.

5

This is the ace from the top of the deck, not the "policeman". No-one should notice as they are both red.

CLOSE-UP CARDS 1

The Glimpse

It is often useful to know the bottom card of the deck. To Glimpse it, ask a spectator to shuffle; if the deck is handed back face-up, you will see the bottom card. If not, square the deck on the table and glance at it then.

Only turn the cards slightly towards you.

Card Spread and Flourish

How to spread cards in your hands is shown on page 31. The top two pictures here show a spread to do on a table. Read how to do it on the right. Practice until you can do it evenly. Then add the flourish in the bottom picture.

Do As I Do

You use two decks of cards, and the Glimpse and Spread techniques above in this trick. Place the decks on a table and ask a volunteer to take one and copy you exactly. Pick up your pack and start shuffling. Then follow these steps, shown from the magician's point of view.

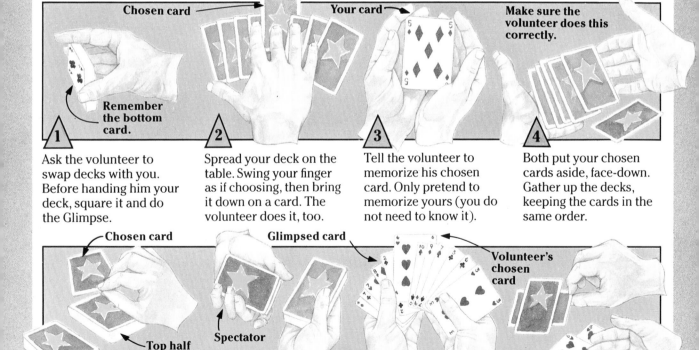

Chosen card · **Your card** · **Make sure the volunteer does this correctly.**

Remember the bottom card.

1
Ask the volunteer to swap decks with you. Before handing him your deck, square it and do the Glimpse.

2
Spread your deck on the table. Swing your finger as if choosing, then bring it down on a card. The volunteer does it, too.

3
Tell the volunteer to memorize his chosen card. Only pretend to memorize yours (you do not need to know it).

4
Both put your chosen cards aside, face-down. Gather up the decks, keeping the cards in the same order.

Chosen card · **Glimpsed card** · **Volunteer's chosen card**

Top half · **Bottom half** · **Spectator** · **Magician**

5
Both cut your decks on the table. Put your chosen card on the top half before completing the cut. Now cut again.

6
Swap decks again. Tell the volunteer to search the pack, find the card he memorized and take it out.

7
Meanwhile, you search for the Glimpsed card and take the one on top of it. Try to finish before the volunteer.

8
Put both cards face-down on the table, one crossways on top of the other. Turn both over. They are the same.

The cards make an overlapping line.

The Spread

◄ Touch the short edges of the deck with your right fingers and thumb. Tap the left side of the cards with your first finger and sweep them to the right.

The Flourish

◄ With your left hand, flip the card on the left face-up. A chain reaction turns all the cards over with a ripple.

Key Card Control

A Control is a way of getting a card to where you want it in the deck. In this Control, you use a Key Card to find an unknown card and bring it to the top. You can use it in many tricks.

1. Glimpse the bottom card. It is the Key Card.

2. Spread the deck and have a card chosen.

3. Cut the deck in two, have the chosen card placed on the top half, then complete the cut.

4. Get the spectator to cut the deck a few times. The Key Card stays with the chosen one.

5. Spread the deck face-up and say something like, "Your card is lost somewhere in here, would you agree?" as an excuse for looking.

6. Spot the Key Card. The chosen card is on top of it.

7. Take the chosen card and those above it in one hand and the Key Card and those below it in the other. Cut the half with the chosen card to the top. Keep talking to misdirect.

Take these cards in one hand and cut them to the top.   **Take these cards in your other hand.**

Chosen card

Key card

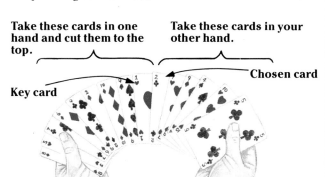

Turn-Around Card

Start with steps 1 to 4 of the Key Card Control (see left) so that the chosen card is next to the Key Card. Now ask the spectator to watch.

Start to deal the cards (take them off the deck one at a time) onto the table, turning them face-up. When you see the Key Card, remember the card that follows it (the chosen card). Deal a few more cards.

Now take a card as if to deal it but don't turn it over. Say that the next card you turn over will be the chosen one. Ask the spectator if he believes you. He should say no, as he has already seen his card dealt.

The spectator assumes you will turn over the card in your hand, so should insist you are wrong. Argue a bit, then replace the held card on the pack, look among the dealt cards, find the chosen one and turn it face-down.

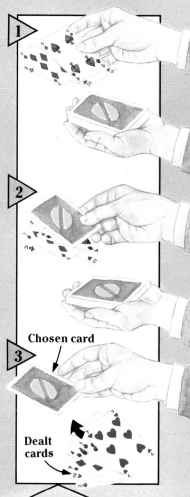

Chosen card

Dealt cards

Sucker tricks

A trick like Turn-Around Card is called a "sucker" trick because it makes the spectator look silly. He is convinced that you will be proved wrong, but you turn the tables. Don't use too many sucker tricks or appear too pleased when you do, or the audience may be offended. It is only a joke, so treat it lightly.

Forces

A Force is a way of making sure that a spectator chooses a particular card. Two kinds of Force are shown below. There are lots of others. If you genuinely allow the spectator a totally free choice of card it is called a "fair selection".

Cut Force

Have the card you want chosen on top of the deck. Ask a spectator to cut the deck in two on the table. Put the bottom half crossways on the top half.

It is important misdirection to let some time pass so everyone forgets what has happened.

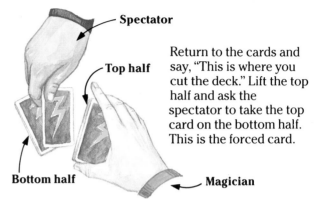

Spectator

Top half

Bottom half

Magician

Return to the cards and say, "This is where you cut the deck." Lift the top half and ask the spectator to take the top card on the bottom half. This is the forced card.

Classic Force

This is considered the best force but it is quite hard and requires some nerve. The best way to practice is to try it out even when a fair selection would do for a trick.

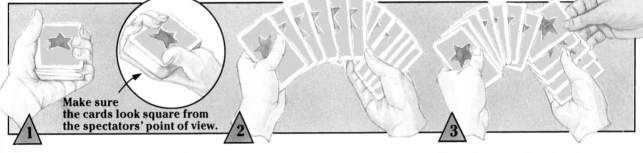

Make sure the cards look square from the spectators' point of view.

1 Glimpse the bottom card. Kick-Cut the deck. As you complete the cut, curl your little finger over the top half. Then put the bottom half on top of it.

2 Spread the cards for a spectator to choose. Your little finger stays trapped in place to keep track of the Glimpsed card.

3 Time the spread so that the Glimpsed card is right under the spectator's fingers as she chooses a card. You will be surprised at how often it works.

Double Lift

Use the Double Lift when you want to seem to show the top card of a deck.

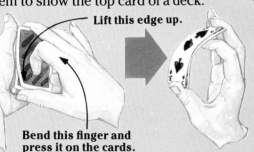

Lift this edge up.

Bend this finger and press it on the cards.

Take the deck in your left hand. Hold the short edges with your right fingers and thumb. With your right thumb, bend up the top two cards and lift them off as one.

Instant Revelation

1 Have a card selected. Then have it returned to the deck and control it to the top by the Shuffle Control.

2 Pick up the deck and show the bottom card to the spectator. Ask casually if this is her card. She should say no.

Shuffle Control

This is another way to get a chosen card to the top of the deck.

1 Start an Overhand Shuffle. About half way through, stop and ask the volunteer to place her card on top of the cards that have already been shuffled.

2 Carry on by shuffling off a single card and letting it fall out of line with the rest of the deck. It should stick out towards you a tiny bit. This is called "in-jogging".

3 Don't pause, but shuffle the rest of the cards normally. Spectators will not notice the in-jogged card. Take the cards below the in-jogged one and cut them to the top. The chosen card is now on the top.

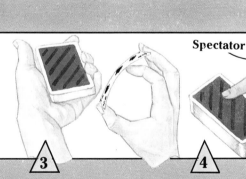

3 Do the Double Lift and show the spectator what appears to be the top card. Ask if this is her card. She will say no. Replace the card(s).

Spectator

4 Hand the deck to the spectator and ask her to tap lightly on the top card. Then tell her to turn it over and she reveals her card.

Countdown

1 Have a card chosen and control it to the top of the deck. Ask a spectator for a number between five and fifteen. Deal that number of cards into a face-down pile.

2 Count the cards out loud as you deal. When you say the last number, turn that card face-up, claiming this is the chosen card. It isn't, so pretend to be puzzled or embarrassed.

Dealt cards

3 Suddenly "realize" that you forgot the magic words, or some similar excuse. Turn the face-up card back over again, pick up all the cards you dealt and put them on top of the deck.

Do a "magic tap".

4 Say some magic words or do something else suitable to correct what was supposed to be your "mistake" in the previous step.

5 Ask the spectator to do the countdown again, just as you did it. This time, when the last card is turned over, it is the correct one. This way the magic "happens" in the spectator's hands, not yours.

Spectator

CLOSE-UP COINS

If you did the French Drop on page 8 you already know one coin slight. Here are some more you should master if you want to do coin tricks. Practice the Palms (palming means to hide in your hand) and Coin Switch before trying the tricks.

Finger Palm

Bend your two middle fingers and hold the coin in them. Let the others curl naturally.

Thumb Palm

1 Hold the coin flat between your first and second fingers.

2 Curl your fingers and pinch the edge of the coin flat between your thumb and palm.

3 Relax your fingers. You cannot move your thumb, but try not to let it look awkward.

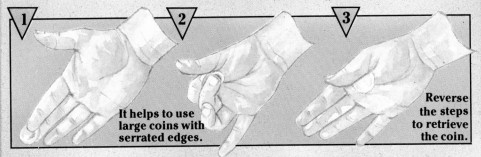

It helps to use large coins with serrated edges.

Reverse the steps to retrieve the coin.

Classic Palm

Press the coin onto your palm with your two middle fingers. Squeeze the fleshy base of your thumb over it to hold it. Straighten your fingers. This is the best Palm, but the hardest to do.

Thumb natural

Fingers free

Thumb Palm Vanish

1 Hold the coin as in step 1, above. Slightly cup your left hand as if you are going to take the coin in it.

2 Put your right fingers into your left hand. Thumb Palm the coin in your right hand while hidden by your left.

3 Move your left hand away as if it has the coin. Relax your right. Now when you open your left hand it is empty.

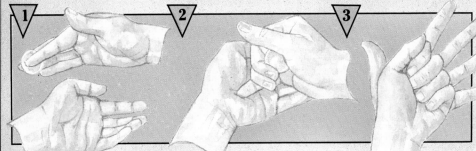

Quick trick

Do a French Drop or Thumb Palm Vanish into your right hand. Show that the coin has gone. Now squeeze your nose with your right hand and let the coin drop into your left.

Copper and Silver

In this trick you make a copper and a silver coin swap places. Take the two coins from a pocket with your right hand. In the same hand, Finger Palm a second copper coin.

Hold up one copper and one silver coin in your fingers. Place the silver one to your left and the copper one to your right on a table in front of you.

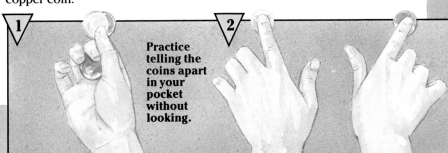

Practice telling the coins apart in your pocket without looking.

Top Pocket Vanish

This is a good trick to confuse people who always think a coin that has vanished must be in the other hand. You need to wear a shirt with a pocket. Do the Thumb Palm Vanish on the page opposite, but don't open your left hand. Then follow these steps.

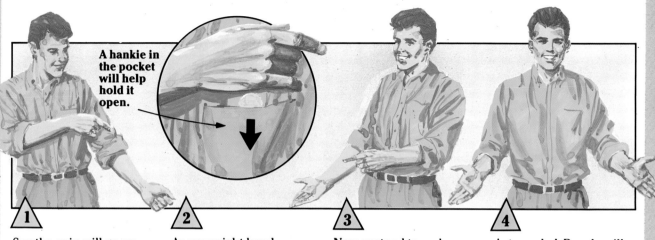

A hankie in the pocket will help hold it open.

1 Say the coin will go up your left arm, across your chest, down your right arm to your right hand. Trace this path with your right finger.

2 As your right hand passes your top pocket, drop the coin into it. Try to do it smoothly and without hesitating in your explanation.

3 Now pretend to make the coin move as described. Follow its supposed path with your eyes. Open your right hand. The coin is not there.

4 Act puzzled. People will assume the coin is still in your left hand. Open that hand, too, to show that the coin has vanished.

Coin Switch

In one hand, Finger Palm a copper coin and hold a silver coin between the first finger and thumb.

Silver coin thrown into right hand.

Silver coin drops into Finger Palm.

1

2 Toss the silver coin into the other hand and close your fingers round it at once. Do it several times.

3 Then make the same motion, but actually toss the copper coin and palm the silver one. Try the Switch from both hands.

Copper coin thrown into right hand.

3 Pick up the silver coin with your right fingers. Say you will hold it in your left hand. Do the Coin Switch from your right to your left hand.

4 Pick up the copper coin on the table with your right fingertips. Tell the spectators to watch carefully.

5 Make a magic gesture. Then let the two coins slide onto the table from the opposite hands to what is expected, as shown in the next step.

6 Let the copper coin slide from your left hand. Simultaneously Thumb Palm the copper coin in your right and release the silver one.

You can do tricks with lots of everyday things, such as dice, a glass or sugar lumps. Each one may not be as versatile as coins or cards, but doing magic with them is effective if you just pick them off a table or borrow them from somebody.

The Paddle Move

The Paddle Move is often done with two small paddle-shaped sticks with spots on. Here you can see how to do it with dice.

1 Take a dice in your first finger and thumb. Have the 6 facing you and the 3 on the face to the left of the 6 as you look at it.

2 Turn your hand to show the face of the dice opposite the 6. Now, the 1 faces you. Reverse the move by turning your hand back again.

These two moves should look identical. If you alternate them, the number on the face opposite the 6 seems to change each time.

3 Turn your hand again, but this time turn the dice round by one face, too, so the 2 is towards you. This is the Paddle Move.

Turn the dice in the same direction as your hand.

Reverse the Paddle Move by turning the dice back round by one face the other way as you turn your hand back.

Dice Swap

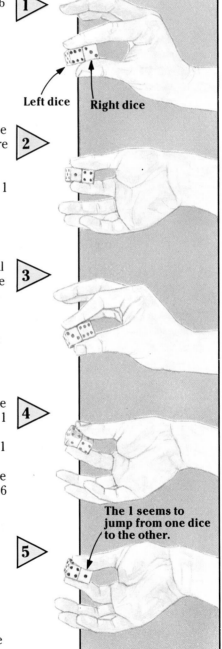

1 Hold two dice like this: left dice has 6 facing you and 3 under your first finger; right dice has 3 facing you and 6 under your finger.

Left dice   Right dice

2 Show the audience the 6 and 3 that are facing you. Turn your hand over normally to show 1 and 4 on the opposite sides.

3 Turn your hand back to its original position, doing the Paddle Move. The audience sees 6 and 3 again (on different dice, but don't point this out).

4 Reverse the Paddle Move to show the 1 and 4 again. Now point out that the 1 is on the left dice. Reverse the Paddle Move to show the 6 and 3 again.

The 1 seems to jump from one dice to the other.

5 Ask people which dice now has 1 on the other side. They should say the left dice. Turn your hand not doing the Paddle Move to reveal the 1 on the right dice.

Sugar Lump Jump

This trick looks good if you can pick some sugar lumps from a bowl on the table. To make it easier to follow, the directions are written in a kind of code. Here is the key to it:

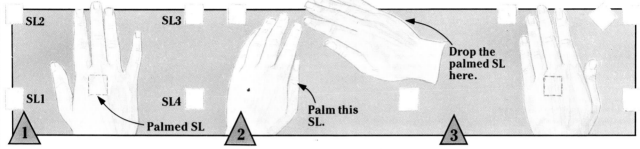

1 Classic Palm (see page 36) one SL in your RH. Place four more SL on a table as shown above. Number them in your head.

2 Cover SL1 with your LH and SL3 with your RH. Release the palmed SL and Classic Palm SL1 in your left hand.

3 Lift your hands to reveal two SL at position 3 and none at 1. You now have a SL palmed in your left hand. Carry on as below.

In each step, drop the palmed SL and palm the other:

4. LH over SL3; RH over SL4.
5. RH over SL3; LH over SL2.

6. Take all the SL in LH (with palmed SL) and replace in bowl.

Glass Through Table

For this trick you need to be sitting at a table. You use a small tumbler glass (without a stem) and a paper napkin. These things may be on the table, if it is set for a meal.

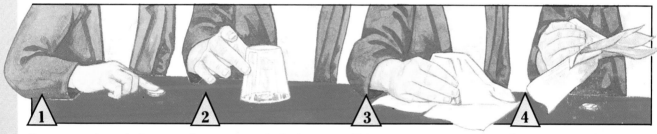

1 Borrow a coin and place it near the edge of the table. Claim you are going to make it pass through the table.

2 Say you must hide the coin and turn the glass over on top of it. As it is see-through, say you must cover it up.

3 Take a paper napkin and drape it over the glass. Mould it firmly round the shape of the glass.

4 Say some magic words and lift the napkin and glass up. The coin is still there. Act upset and replace the glass.

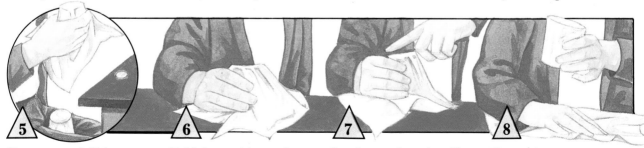

5 Repeat step 4, lifting napkin and glass over the edge of the table. Drop the glass unseen into your lap.

6 Hold the napkin gently to keep the glass shape. The coin is still there. Say you will try again. Put the napkin over it.

7 Say that as the coin will not perform properly, you will make the glass do it instead (people think it is still there).

8 Flatten the napkin with one hand and bring the glass out from under the table with the other.

SILENT MAGIC: CARD MANIPULATION

Many magicians who work silently use manipulation. This is the art of handling small props with great dexterity and performing tricks purely by slight of hand. On the next six pages you can learn basic manipulation skills with cards, coins, billiard balls and thimbles. They are quite hard and take a long time to perfect, but don't be put off. Practicing and improving is enjoyable in itself.

The Thumb Fan

1 Hold the deck of cards in your left hand, clasped between your thumb and palm.

2 Put your right thumb against the top left edge and push the cards to the right. Push the cards on the bottom of the pile first.

This works best with a slippery new deck of cards.

3 Run your right thumb across the tops of the cards in a curve to make a fan. The cards swivel under your left thumb.

The Back Palm

This card palm is basic to card manipulation. Follow the steps below to vanish and re-produce a card. You must blend the individual steps into a smooth, rapid action.

The vanish

1 Hold a card upright by the bottom right corner between your first two fingers and thumb.

2 Use your fingers to swivel the card horizontal.

The card is held curved behind your hand.

3 As it comes horizontal, put your first finger along the top long edge and your little finger along the bottom one.

Do both moves with a swift up and down gesture. It hides the slight and looks as though you toss the card into thin air or pluck it from nowhere.

Work on stopping the corners poking out.

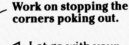

5 Let go with your thumb, straighten your fingers and clip the corners of the card between your first and second and third and fourth fingers. It disappears behind your hand.

4 Curl your second and third fingers towards your palm and push them against the short edge of the card to flip it over.

The re-production

6 To re-produce the card, keep your first finger straight but bend the others so that you can grab the corner of the card with your thumb.

Springing the Deck

This is an impressive flourish but is quite difficult. Practice over your bed or into a box to stop the cards flying everywhere.

Hands close together

▷**1** Hold the deck by its short edges. Bend it in towards your palm. Put your other hand beneath

▽**2** Release cards one by one and catch them. As you get better at it, move your hands apart.

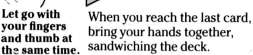

Let go with your fingers and thumb at the same time.

▷**3** When you reach the last card, bring your hands together, sandwiching the deck.

Back Palming several cards

Once you can palm one card, put another in the same hand and follow steps 1-5 again. Slip the second card on top of the first. Build up until you can palm six or so at once.

Re-produce them by following steps 6-8, releasing only one card at a time. The hardest part is to keep hold of the palmed cards while you take or release another.

◁**8** Continue to pull the card out with your thumb. Move your first finger out of the way so it can flip upright in front of your fingers.

◁**7** Press down with your thumb and release the card from between your third and fourth fingers.

Basic Back Palm Routine

In this pose you can do the moves without revealing how.

△**1** Hold six cards in a small fan in your left hand. Stand with your left shoulder to the audience.

△**2** Take a card in your right hand. Pretend to toss it into the air, making it vanish using the Back Palm.

△**3** Repeat five times. You could look astonished as the cards vanish, or act as if it is perfectly normal.

△**4** After a pause, pretend to see something in the air, reach out and re-produce a card, as if from nowhere.

△**5** Take the re-produced card with your left hand. Or you could just let it drop onto the floor or a table.

△**6** Repeat until all six cards reappear. Make "seeing" the cards before you grab them as convincing as possible.

41

SILENT MAGIC: COIN MANIPULATION

Many coin tricks involve vanishing coins and re-producing them in an unusual way. The Miser's Dream, below, is probably the best-known one that can be performed silently on stage. To do it you need to learn the Edge Palm slight shown here.

The Edge Palm

This palm is sometimes called the Downs Palm after the American magician T. Nelson Downs, who invented it.

The coin is still flat.

View from on top.

View from the side.

1 Hold a coin flat between your first and second fingers.

2 Curl your fingers to put the coin in the crook of your thumb. Grip it between your thumb and first finger.

3 Keeping hold of the coin, straighten your fingers naturally. In the two pictures above you can see what it should look like to you from the side and from on top.

4 To re-produce the coin, Curl your fingers in and take it between your first and second fingers.

5 Straighten your fingers to reveal the coin held at the tips.

Make the coins disappear with a tossing motion. This helps hide the slight and makes it seem as if you throw the coins into thin air.

Talking coins

In coin tricks, if coins clink when they should not it is called "talking".

It may seem difficult to avoid talk at first, especially when handling more than one coin (see opposite), but keep trying and it will come.

The Miser's Dream

It is easiest to prepare this trick before coming on stage, so it is a good one to do first. In the trick, you seem to pluck coins from thin air to toss into a bucket. You can't Edge Palm enough coins for the whole trick, so after the first three you fool people with an illusion.

Practice "seeing" a coin in empty air.

The bucket is shown transparent here so you can see.

1 To prepare, Edge Palm 4 coins in your right hand. Hide 10 coins in your left hand, as shown above.

2 Pick up a bucket or tin with your left hand, as shown. Now you are ready. You seem just to be holding an empty bucket.

3 "See" a coin in mid-air. Reach for it, draw a coin from the Edge-Palm, display it and toss it in the bucket. Repeat twice.

Edge Palming lots of coins

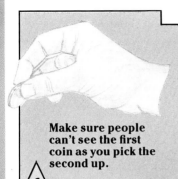

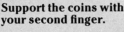

Support the coins with your second finger.

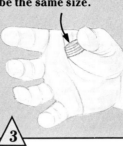

The coins must all be the same size.

Make sure people can't see the first coin as you pick the second up.

1
With one coin already held in the Edge Palm (see left), pick up another with your first finger and thumb.

2
Put it between your first and second fingers. Then curl these fingers and slide the second coin under the first.

3
Grip both coins and straighten your fingers as before. Repeat with as many coins as you are able to hold.

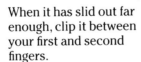

4
To re-produce coins one at a time, curl your second finger in under the stack of coins and slip the bottom one out.

5
When it has slid out far enough, clip it between your first and second fingers.

6
Straighten your fingers, with the coin held at the tips. Don't forget to keep gripping the coins that are still palmed.

Stealing and loads

Manipulators often need to get more props secretly while performing. This is called "stealing".

The prop you steal is called a "load". If it is attached to yourself, it is a "body-load". Loads can also be fixed to a table or chair. Always fix a body load to a part of your clothing that does not move. A jacket can swing, for instance, but trousers stay in the same place.

Pin the load somewhere hidden.

This picture shows a clip for holding cards to be stolen during an act. You can make one simply using a paper clip with a safety pin stuck through it.

The clink of the coin you drop makes people think you really threw another coin.

4
Take the last Edge Palmed coin and pretend to toss it in too, but really, re-palm it and drop a coin from your left hand.

5
Repeat step 4 nine times. You produce and Edge Palm the same coin each time and let a coin drop from your left hand with a clink. Be inventive about "finding" coins. You could pretend to make a spectator "catch" an invisible coin and throw it into the bucket.

6
Or produce a coin from a spectator's lapel or behind his ear, for example. Ideas like these add variety.

7
At the end, show all the coins in the bucket. This "proves" that you really threw them all in, in case people were suspicious.

MANIPULATING BILLIARD BALLS

Manipulating billiard balls is quite hard, especially if your hands are small. You can buy special balls in magic shops, which are lighter and easier to handle.

Ball Roll Flourish

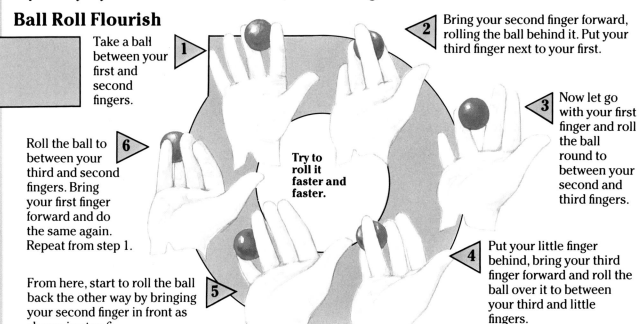

1 Take a ball between your first and second fingers.

2 Bring your second finger forward, rolling the ball behind it. Put your third finger next to your first.

3 Now let go with your first finger and roll the ball round to between your second and third fingers.

4 Put your little finger behind, bring your third finger forward and roll the ball over it to between your third and little fingers.

5 From here, start to roll the ball back the other way by bringing your second finger in front as shown in step 6.

6 Roll the ball to between your third and second fingers. Bring your first finger forward and do the same again. Repeat from step 1.

Try to roll it faster and faster.

Billiard ball slights

These pictures show how slights you already know (pages 8 and 36) work with a billiard ball.

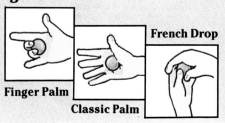

Finger Palm

Classic Palm

French Drop

Swallowing the Ball

Do a French Drop to leave the ball in your right hand. Lift your left hand and pretend to eat the ball. Rub your stomach with your right hand and re-produce it.

Bottom of Fist Vanish

When you practice this slight, make the move for real first, (a rehearsal technique suggested on page 16), to feel how the ball's weight affects your movements.

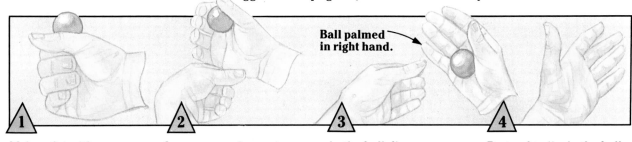

Ball palmed in right hand.

1 Make a fist with your right hand. Balance the ball on top of it.

2 Loosen your fingers to let the ball drop into your hand. Hold your left hand as if to catch it underneath.

3 As the ball disappears, close your left hand and move it down and away as if the ball has dropped into it.

4 Pretend to jiggle the ball in your left hand, then open your hand to show the ball has gone.

MANIPULATING THIMBLES

Thimbles are also frequently used by manipulators. Because they are small and light, they are easier to practise with than billiard balls. See how to make a thimble holder on page 58.

Thumb Palm

Practice putting the thimble in the Thumb Palm from your second and third fingers, too.

1 Place a thimble on your first finger. Hold your hand outstretched.

2 Curl your first finger into the crook of your thumb and take the thimble between your thumb and palm.

3 Straighten your finger, leaving the thimble held by your thumb. It is completely hidden.

Thumb Palm Vanish

Try to make the steps look like one continuous movement.

Palming thimble

1 Rest the first finger of your right hand, wearing the thimble, on the open palm of your left hand.

2 Turn your left hand over to hide the thimble. Quickly thumb palm it and straighten your finger again.

3 Curl your left hand round your finger and slide it up and off as if pulling the thimble from your fingertip.

4 A moment or two later, you can open your left hand to show that the thimble has vanished.

Jumping Thimbles

This trick uses two identical thimbles and the Thumb Palm to make it look as if a thimble is jumping from one hand to the other.

Here you are looking at the magician's hands.

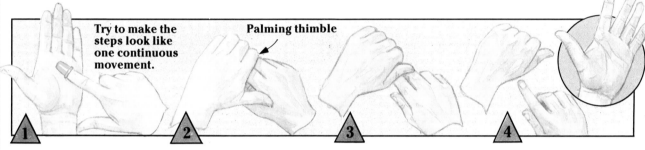

The movement of your hands hides the slight.

Swing your hands back and forth, doing the slight each time.

The thimble seems to have jumped to your other hand.

1 Thumb palm a thimble in your left hand. The other is on your right first finger. Hold both hands at waist level, pointing down and right.

2 Swing your hands to the left, Thumb Palming the thimble on your right finger and retrieving the other with your left first finger as you move.

3 Straighten your fingers as your hands stop. You now have a thimble on your left first finger and one Thumb Palmed in your right hand.

4 Swing your hands back to the right, Palming the thimble on your left hand and retrieving the one in your right.

CABARET MAGIC

In cabaret, an interesting presentation is as important as technical skill. On the next four pages are some well-known cabaret tricks. Do them all, select those you particularly enjoy and try to think of your own way of presenting them.

Afghan Bands

In this trick, three seemingly identical loops of paper are cut in the same way, with odd results. You need three strips of paper 1-2ins wide and 39ins long; glue and scissors.

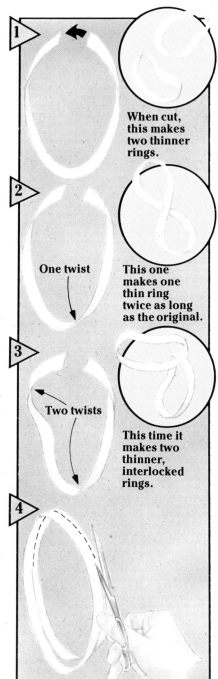

To prepare the first strip, put a dab of glue on one end of it. Bring the other end round and stick it flat on the gluey bit to make a loop.

1

When cut, this makes two thinner rings.

Do it again with the second strip, only this time twist the band once by turning your hand before you stick it down.

2

One twist

This one makes one thin ring twice as long as the original.

Repeat with the third band, but this time twist the end twice before you stick it down flat.

3

Two twists

This time it makes two thinner, interlocked rings.

Cut each ring in half along its length. Push the point of the scissors through the middle of the band then cut all the way round as shown here by the dotted line.

4

Presentation ideas

Take a theme of wedding rings. Write the names of couples in the audience on each band. Cut between the names. Make joking remarks about the couples according to how the rings turn out. You could say the linked rings showed a very close couple, for example. Don't say anything rude or unpleasant.

Jane
Geoff

Or start by saying you need more rings for this trick and ask a volunteer to help you cut them. Tell her to copy you exactly. You cut two straight rings, but give her two twisted ones. You can make a joke when her rings don't turn out right.

Cabaret tips

- *Display props at waist height or higher and make sure they can be seen by the whole audience.*

- *Avoid tricks that must be seen from one angle only.*

- *If you put a prop on a table, ensure people can see it all the time or they may suspect you of switching (changing the prop for another that looks identical).*

Cut and Restored Rope

For this trick you will need a piece of rope about 4ft long and a sharp pair of scissors. In magic shops, you can buy special rope that cuts easily, but you can use ordinary rope.

1 Take hold of the rope between your left finger and thumb near one end (called A in the picture).

2 Pick up the other end (B) and place it next to A, sticking up by the same amount above your left hand.

3 Take the bottom of the rope loop with your first and second right fingers. Lift it up towards the ends in your left hand.

4 Put your right thumb through the loop and grab end B just below your left thumb.

5 Pull some rope up through the loop with your right first finger and thumb to make a fake loop.

6 Let go with your right hand as you take the base of the fake loop in your left hand. Hide the join with your thumb.

7 Say you will now cut the rope. Cut the fake loop. Now you have four ends, A,B,C and D sticking out above your left thumb.

8 Drop ends A and D. (When you practice, you may need to look under your left thumb to check which end is which.)

9 You now seem to have two pieces of rope. Say you will make them one again and tie a single knot with ends B and C.

10 Display the knotted rope. People should laugh at this phoney magic. Say you will get rid of the knot.

11 Hide the knot with your left hand. Snip bits off the short ends and let them fall. Then snip the knot itself off the rope.

12 Take end D in your right hand and slowly pull the rope out of your left hand to show it restored.

47

Coin in Wool

For this trick you need some wool, a tumbler glass and a cardboard tube, which you can make yourself. See how to prepare the trick on the right. Then follow steps 1 to 6, below, to see how to present it. It helps if your glass is lightly coloured, or patterned, so it is not so easy to see through.

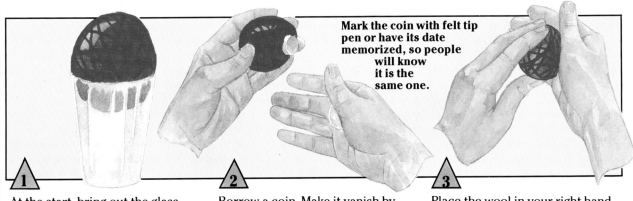

Leave this end open.

Totally cover this end.

▲

Take a piece of thin cardboard about 3ins by 1.25ins Bend the two short sides round to meet each other.

▲

Overlap the short ends by about 0.5ins and stick with glue or tape. Paint it to match the wool you use.

▲

Hold the tube on your finger. Wind wool round it until it looks like a ball. Don't wind it too tightly.

Mark the coin with felt tip pen or have its date memorized, so people will know it is the same one.

1

At the start, bring out the glass with the wool on top. The open end of the tube sticks down into the glass so the audience will not see it.

2

Borrow a coin. Make it vanish by doing a Thumb Palm Vanish (or use the Hankie Vanish on the right). Pick up the wool with your left hand.

3

Place the wool in your right hand, putting the open end of the tube directly over the palmed coin. This frees your left hand to lift the glass.

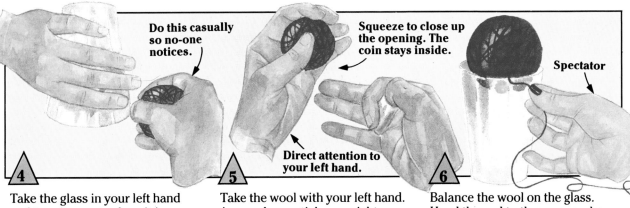

Do this casually so no-one notices.

Squeeze to close up the opening. The coin stays inside.

Spectator

Direct attention to your left hand.

4

Take the glass in your left hand and turn it over to show it is empty. At the same time, turn your right hand over so the coin drops into the tube.

5

Take the wool with your left hand. As you do so, stick your right thumb in the tube, pull it out of the wool and Thumb Palm it in your right hand.

6

Balance the wool on the glass. Hand the end to the person who gave you the coin to pull gently. As the wool unwinds, the coin drops into the glass.

Hankie Vanish

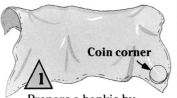

1 Prepare a hankie by opening the hem at one corner and inserting a small coin. Then sew it up again.

Hold the coin corner.

2 To do the Vanish, take a similar coin in your right hand. With your left hand, drape the hankie over it.

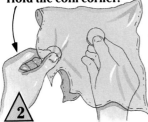

3 Take the coin corner up underneath into the center of the hankie. Thumb Palm the real coin in your right hand.

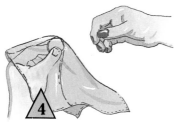

4 Ask someone to hold the sewn-in coin through the hankie. When you whisk the hankie from him, the coin vanishes.

Two Card Trick

You need a box deep enough to turn cards over in without being seen, and two decks of cards.

To prepare the trick, choose two contrasting cards, such as the two of diamonds (2D) and the ten of spades (10S). Take both cards out of both decks. Take the two cards from one of the decks and stick them back to back. This is called a "double-facer".

Ten of spades.

1 Start with the double-facer in your right pocket, with the 10S facing away from you. Openly take the 10S and 2D from the complete pack and put them in the box on a table.

2 Explain that you will put a card in your pocket (do it with the 10S to show them) and they must guess which card is left. Now bring out the double-facer, showing the 10S.

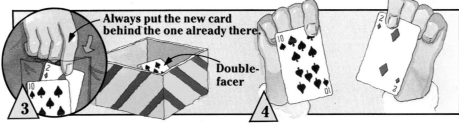

3 Put the double-facer (10S side up) in the box and say that now you will start for real. Take the 2D from the box, show it briefly and put it in your pocket.

4 Ask which card is in the box. They will say the 10S. In the box, turn the double-facer to the 2D side then show it to the audience. Take the 10S from your pocket.

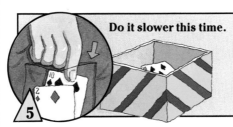

5 Say you will try again. Put both cards in the box. Turn the double-facer, show its 10S side and put it in your pocket. They will be sure the 2D is left.

6 Slowly reach in the box and take out the 10S. Then take the 2D from your pocket. Throw both cards in the box and hand it out for inspection.

MENTALISM

Mentalists pretend to use mind-reading, telepathy (sending thoughts from one person to another) and other mental powers. You need confidence to do tricks like these and it helps to have a good memory and a knack for quick thinking.

Specialists

Most specialists like to imply that their powers are real, but are careful not to claim they can definitely predict the future.

They tend not to mix other kinds of tricks in their act.

Slapstick humour does not seem appropriate. Subtle humour may be used.

Some cultivate unusual looks or behavior that will get them noticed.

Book Test

For this trick you need a few books. Then follow these steps:

1 Ask a spectator to pick a book and give it to you.

2 Casually flip the pages. Near the middle, memorize a page number and the first word on the page.

3 Hand the book to the spectator.

4 Ask the spectator for another book.

It can be effective to get the word slightly wrong – say "ever" if the word is "clever", for example. Claim you can't quite read the whole thought.

5 Take this book and flip the pages. Tell the spectator to say stop at any time. You must make sure you are somewhere near the middle when he does.

6 Pretend to look at then say the page number you stopped at. Actually, say the memorized number.

7 Close the book at once and carry on.

8 Ask the spectator to look at that page number in his book and memorize the first word.

9 Tell him to concentrate on the word so you can read his mind.

10 Pause for effect, then say the memorized word.

Newspaper Prediction

In this trick, you "predict" where a spectator will tell you to cut a newspaper column. The spectator seems to have a free choice, but you arrange things as described in steps 1 to 3 first. Steps 4 to 7 explain how to present the trick. The column must all be in the same type size, except for the headline.

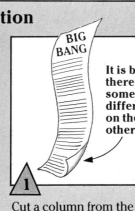

It is best if there is something different on the other side.

People will not be close enough to see the join.

The line you write is here.

1 Cut a column from the day's newspaper. It should have a headline big enough to read from a distance.

2 Cut off the headline. Cut the top and bottom off the column and turn it upside-down. Stick the headline back on to it.

3 Write out the line of type furthest from the headline. This is your "prediction". Put it in a sealed envelope.

Personality Probe

The method for this trick is simple. It needs good misdirection and a confident presentation to succeed. Some hints are given below.

Tips on mentalism

One or two mentalist tricks can be very effective in any act. Here are some hints about including them:

- *Don't talk about a trick. Say "test" or "experiment".*

- *Be slightly wrong now and then. A guess which is close but not quite right adds authenticity.*

- *If a coincidence or unusual thing happens, claim you planned it.*

- *You will find certain things are likely, such as that people often say 3 if asked for a number between 1 and 5, for example.*

- *Invent scientific "facts" about your powers. They don't have to be true.*

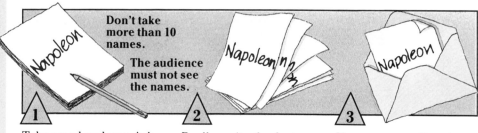

Don't take more than 10 names.

The audience must not see the names.

1 Take a pad and pen. Ask people to call out the names of famous people. Pretend to write each name on a new page, tear it off and put it on the table.

2 Really, write the first name given on each sheet. To misdirect, ask someone to repeat a name, as if you did not hear it. Ask another to spell a tricky name.

3 Now say you will make a prediction. Write the first name on another sheet of paper. Put this sheet in an envelope and seal it. Give it to a spectator to hold.

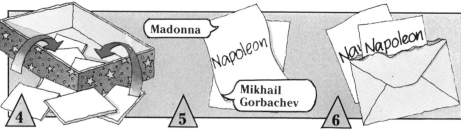

Madonna

Mikhail Gorbachev

4 Fold all the bits of paper you have written on and put them in a box. Shake them around then get another spectator to pick one out. Place the box aside.

5 Take one or two papers from the box and pretend to read names that were called out earlier. This should convince people that the papers are genuine.

6 Ask the spectator who picked a paper to read the name on it and the one with the envelope to open it and read your prediction. The names are the same.

BIG BANG

Memorize a couple of sentences if you cannot read upside-down.

The audience assumes the column is the right way up.

Let the cut paper fall to the floor.

When it is the right way up, the top line is the one you copied out.

4 Have some scissors ready. Hold up the column and read a bit aloud. Give a spectator the prediction to hold.

5 Say you will run the scissors up and down the column and cut wherever a chosen spectator says stop.

6 Do it, then hand the cut piece to the spectator and ask him to read the top line. He will turn it the right way up.

7 Ask the spectator holding your prediction to open it and read it out. It will be exactly the same line.

CHILDREN'S MAGIC

This kind of magic is usually performed for children of about four to eight years old. It is often part of a birthday party.

Joking, having lots of fun and letting the children join in are more important than doing complicated tricks.

Hello Routine

This is not a trick, but should get you off to a good start. The children get to know you and get used to joining in.

At the start say,

> I'm rather shy so would you please say hello when I say hello to you?

Walk away, then come back. Someone is bound to shout hello. Say,

> No, no that's wrong. Wait until I say hello first.

Go off and come back again. There should be silence. Wait a bit, then start to look ill at ease. They expect you to speak. You say,

> Sorry, I've forgotton what I'm supposed to say.

They will almost certainly shout hello, to remind you. Look relieved and say,

> Thank you.

Then go off and come back, saying,

> Hello.

You should get a very loud hello in return.

Farmyard Noises

You could trace pictures or cut them out of magazines.

Double-facer

Pin this one to you.

For this trick you need to make six cards, as shown here. They all have the same back (a farm, say) except one. This is a double-facer with a duplicate cow on one side and horse on the other. Pile the cards face-up in the above order (horse on the top, question mark on the bottom). Pin the cow card to your back.

1 Square the cards and hold them up showing the horse. Ask the children what noise a horse makes and tell them to make it.

2 Put the horse card at the back and show the pig. Ask them to make the right noise. Put it at the back. Do the same with the sheep.

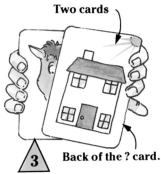

Two cards

Back of the ? card.

3 Now introduce the cow as Daisy. Say she's shy and will turn her back. Do a Double Lift (page 34) and turn Daisy and the question mark around.

This is the double-facer.

4 Turn the top card over, showing the question mark. Say it seems that Daisy has gone. Ask the children where she could be.

5 Start to look round for her. Ask the children to help. When you turn your back they will see the other Daisy and will shout out.

6 Pretend not to understand. Turn around comically, looking. Eventually, "realize" what they are saying and "find" the card.

Colorful Silks

You need four silk scarves: two medium sized ones (one red and one yellow); a small one and a big one, both half red and half yellow. You also need a colorful tube, open at both ends, to put them in.

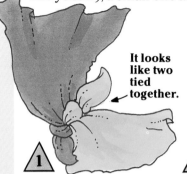

It looks like two tied together.

1
To prepare the trick, tie the small silk round the big silk where the two colors meet. Use a loose single knot.

The tube is shown cut away so you can see inside.

2
Hide the knotted silks in the tube, red half near one end and yellow half near the other. You are now ready.

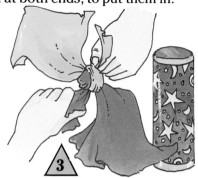

3
To prepare, tie the small silk round the big one where the colors on the big silk meet. Use a loose, single knot.

4
Stuff the medium silks into the tube, the same way as the hidden silk (the same colors towards the same ends.)

People think these are the two ends of the tied medium silks.

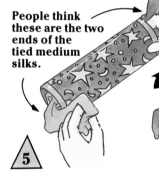

5
As you do, push the hidden silk down and pull out its yellow corner. Leave some red showing at the top.

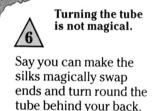

Turning the tube is not magical.

6
Say you can make the silks magically swap ends and turn round the tube behind your back. There will be protests.

7
Say you will do another trick. Push the red end into the tube and pull the yellow end to remove the big silk.

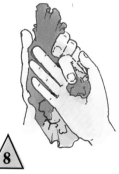

8
Rumple it up into your left hand. As you do so, secretly undo the small silk and palm it in your right hand.

It looks like the two medium silks joined into a big two-colored one.

9
Fetch a wand from your pocket with your right hand. Leave the palmed silk there. Wave the wand and open the big silk.

ESCAPOLOGY

Not many magicians specialize in escapology. It is more often used as a publicity stunt or as one part of an act.

Spectacular escapes are often dangerous and should only be attempted by experienced professionals.

Sack Escape

For this escape you need a big canvas sack with eyelets around the top, through which to thread a rope, and an assistant to put up a screen. *

 1 Pick a volunteer. Climb into the sack. As you crouch down, pull down inside with you a loop of rope about 13ins long.

 2 Ask the volunteer to tie the rope securely. You must hold the loop tightly.

 3 Have the screen put in front of you. Let go of the loop and you have room to get your hands out to undo the knots and escape.

The thicker the rope, the harder it is to tie tightly.

Never use a plastic bag or sack in this trick.

Tips on escapology

- *Rehearse in harder conditions than necessary, with help nearby. Then you should be able to cope if things go wrong on stage.*

- *Check props rigorously.*

- *Brief helpers with extra care.*

- *Make it look harder than it is. Expend lots of energy; wince and groan as if it hurts.*

Rope Escape

This escape requires a scarf or handkerchief, a rope and a volunteer. On stage, you might use a screen, but it works just as well using a jacket to hide your hands.

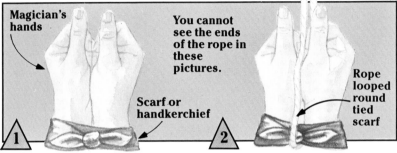

Magician's hands

You cannot see the ends of the rope in these pictures.

Scarf or handkerchief

Rope looped round tied scarf

1 Have your wrists tied. Try to get room to manouvre by twisting your wrists so they are not quite flat together.

2 Get a volunteer to put the rope between your arms and hold both ends. Make him move away from you a bit.

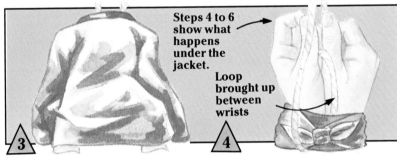

Steps 4 to 6 show what happens under the jacket.

Loop brought up between wrists

3 Have a jacket thrown over your hands. The helper still holds the rope ends. (With a screen, the helper stays in front.)

4 Wriggle your wrists to bring the loop of rope that is between your arms up through the tied scarf and between your wrists.

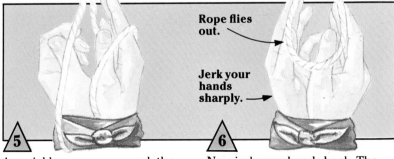

Rope flies out.

Jerk your hands sharply.

5 As quickly as you can, work the loop up and over one hand. Let it fall slack to the outside.

6 Now jerk your hands back. The rope slips out under the handkerchief and you escape. Your hands are still tied.

Make absolutely sure your assistant knows the signal you will give if you are in trouble.

ILLUSIONS

Illusions are exciting to perform but the cost of equipment, the difficulty of transporting it, caring for live animals and the need to employ assistants are all potential problems. It can even be hard to find venues to perform some big illusions.

Pushmi-Pullu

This illusion does not involve buying anything except a rope. You do, however, need two people to help you and a stage to perform on. The stage must have wings on each side (areas to walk off into, out of sight of the audience) and a means of getting from one side to the other without being seen. Your acting skills are also important to make it look effective.

One assistant is in the wings holding the rope. You walk on stage from this side, dragging the rope over your shoulder as if you are pulling a heavy weight on the end.

Go across the stage and off the other side. Give the second assistant the rope to keep pulling so it looks as if you carry on walking. Run unseen back to the first side.

Take the end of the rope from the first assistant and let the second pull you on stage. This gives the illusion that the heavy weight you were pulling was yourself.

Lean back against the pull of the rope to make it as realistic as you can. Let yourself be pulled off the other side before returning to take a bow.

Tips on illusions

- *Most illusions must be bought from a magic dealer or specially made.*

- *Learn to handle all parts of the illusion smoothly.*

- *Don't let the preparation drag.*

- *Costumes, scenery, props and lighting should be carefully thought out to enhance the effect.*

- *Try to ensure that the audience thinks you, rather than the prop, are responsible for the illusion.*

QUICK EFFECTS

The effects on these two pages are most startling done casually. Don't build them up as big tricks but do them in passing, when you happen to have the prop to hand.

Jumping Match

Hold a safety match tightly near its head end in your left first finger and thumb. Put your second fingernail under it and press down hard against that, too. *

It can be hard to get the right effect at first. Keep practicing.

 Balance a second match on the first, as shown. Let it rest lightly on your right first finger.

Match rubs against nail.

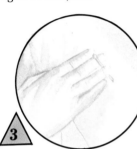

Say you will fill the second match with static electricity. Rub it on your sleeve then replace it.

Now if you move the first match slightly, the friction against your fingernail causes a twitch making the second match leap.

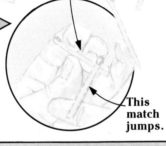

This match jumps.

Twangy Band

Out of sight, put an elastic band over your first two right fingers. Pull it towards you with your left first finger.

Do these secretly.

Curl all your right fingers, put them inside the elastic, then release it so they are all enclosed. Now you are ready.

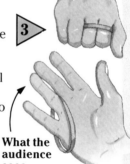

Hold up your fist to show the band round the first two fingers. Uncurl your fingers and it jumps to the third and fourth ones.

What the audience sees.

Rubber Pencil

Hold the pencil loosely in your first finger and thumb. Twist your wrist rapidly round one way and back the other, making the pencil wag.

This gives the illusion that the pencil bends.

Stretching Silk

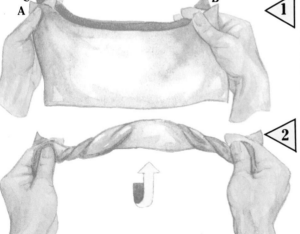

Fold a silk in two, as shown. Hold corners A and B between your thumbs and first fingers; and hold C and D between your first and second fingers.

Make small circles with your hands towards yourself to twirl the silk around itself. You could now consider and say the silk should be a bit longer.

You are now holding the silk diagonally.

Let go of corners A and D. Hold onto B and C and keep twirling. Move your hands further apart and the silk seems to stretch.

Dollar Bill Puzzle

You can do this puzzling trick with any bank bill. One with a face or figure on is best as it clearly has a right and wrong way up. You can do it more than once, if you like.

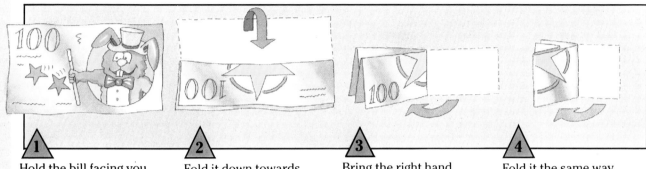

1 Hold the bill facing you. Point out that it is the right way up.

2 Fold it down towards you lengthways.

3 Bring the right hand edges towards you and over onto the left hand edges to fold it in half widthways.

4 Fold it the same way again, taking the right side over to the left.

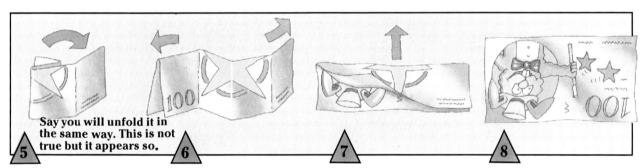

Say you will unfold it in the same way. This is not true but it appears so.

5 Take the open ends of the bill (at the back on the left side) and unfold them away from you and to the right.

6 Take the open end that is now at the back on the right side and unfold it away from you and to the left.

7 Slowly and dramatically, unfold the bill towards you lengthways.

8 It is upside-down, without being turned. If you repeat the trick, do it swiftly so no-one can work it out.

Levitating Matches

You could say some magic words to make the matches stay in, then "undo" the magic to make them fall out.

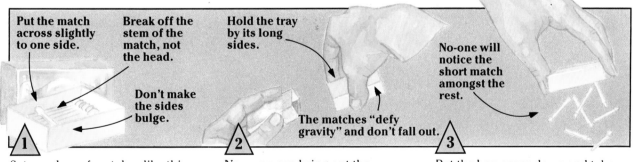

Put the match across slightly to one side.

Break off the stem of the match, not the head.

Don't make the sides bulge.

Hold the tray by its long sides.

The matches "defy gravity" and don't fall out.

No-one will notice the short match amongst the rest.

1 Set up a box of matches like this: break the end off one match so it fits the box width exactly. Place it across the other matches, as shown. *

2 Now you can bring out the matchbox and push the drawer half out to show the matches. Then close it, turn it over and push the tray right out.

3 Put the box cover down and take the tray in your free hand. This time hold it by the short sides and squeeze gently. The matches will now drop out.

Be extra careful when using matches not to light one accidentally.

PROPS TO MAKE

Many magicians like to make their own props so they can tailor them to their needs. Here are some you could make and some ways to use them.

Production tube

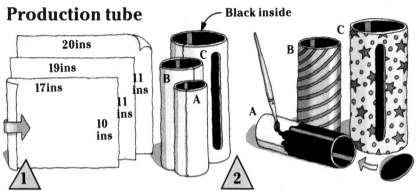

Black inside

Try producing a present or toy rabbit at a children's party.

1 You need three pieces of poster board of about these sizes. Paint one side of each black. Then roll them into tubes and stick down.

2 Stick a circle of poster board on tube A as a bottom. Paint A black. Cut a long hole in tube C. Decorate B and C brightly.

3 To prepare a trick, put a prop in tube A then put A in tube B and B in tube C. Have the tubes upright on your table to start.

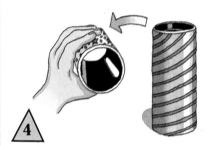

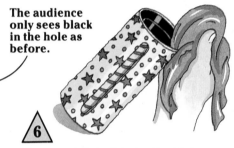

The audience only sees black in the hole as before.

4 Lift tube C off the other two tubes and show the audience it is empty. Then replace it.

5 Draw tube B out from between A and C and show the audience it is empty, too. Now replace it.

6 Now reach into the smallest tube and take your prop out of the "empty" tubes.

Thimble holder

Here is how you can make a holder from which to steal thimbles during an act. Pin it somewhere hidden but within easy reach. Experiment to find the best place.

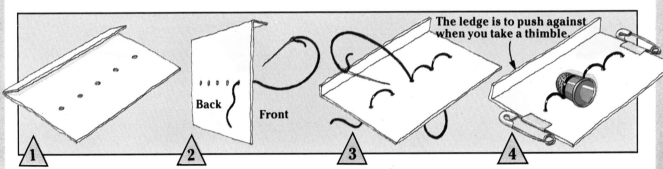

The ledge is to push against when you take a thimble.

Back **Front**

1 Take a piece of strong cardboard and bend one long edge over by about 0.5in. Make five evenly-spaced holes in the card.

2 Thread some narrow elastic through the holes. Start at one end and go in and out of consecutive holes.

3 When you reach the far end, come back the other way. Now you have four loops of elastic on your cardboard.

4 Tie the loose ends in a knot. Tape safety pins to each side of the cardboard. The loops will hold four thimbles.

Foxes and Chickens

Here you can see how to make the props to do the Foxes and Chickens trick underneath. The trick makes use of the fact that you can only see three sides of a cube from any angle. You need to make seven small cubes and prepare two larger boxes.

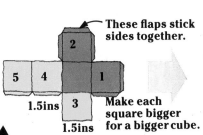

These flaps stick sides together.

5 4 1
2
3

1.5ins

1.5ins

Make each square bigger for a bigger cube.

▲ For each cube, draw a shape like this and cut it out. Paint five of them all blue and the other two half blue and half yellow, as shown above.

Cubes painted like this can look yellow from one angle and blue from the opposite one.

▲ Fold the flaps up, then fold each square up to make a box, starting with square 1. Glue the flaps inside the adjacent sides to hold it together.

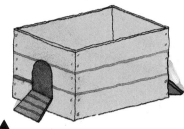

▲ You could paint the bigger boxes like chicken coops. Or just cover them with bright paper or paint.

The trick

The speech bubbles give the story to tell and under the pictures are the moves to make. You see it from the magician's point of view. The two-colored cubes are called YB for short.

These blue cubes are chickens and the yellow ones are foxes.

The chickens live in two coops.

One night two sly foxes came to steal and eat the chickens.

1 Put the boxes and cubes on a table, showing the yellow sides of the YB cubes.

2 Put the blue cubes in alternate boxes one at a time, starting with the box on your right.

3 Put one YB cube in each box.

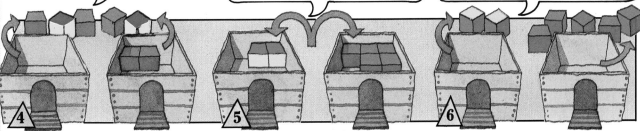

But the chickens heard them coming and ran away.

The foxes hid in the coops and kept quiet so the chickens came back.

It could have been a disaster. But these were very clever chickens. Next day, the farmer found all the chickens in one coop and two foxes trapped in the other.

4 Take five cubes one by one from alternate boxes, starting on your left. Take the YB ones first, turning them to show the blue sides.

5 Put five cubes in the boxes like this: blue to the right, YB to the left, repeat once, then put a blue to the right.

6 Take the cubes out of each box as you speak, showing the yellow side of the YB ones.

MAGIC VARIATIONS

See for yourself how versatile magic can be. Try making each of the varied tricks below suit several styles of act. You will find some help on the page opposite.

Thumb Surprise

The audience seems to see one whole thumb.

Your thumb tip seems removeable.

1
Bend both thumbs and fit them together as shown above.

2
Cover the join with the first two fingers of your right hand.

3
Move your right hand away from your left then together again.

Glasses and Bottles

What you need:

Two dark colored ▶ plastic bottles (they must not be see-through). Cut their bottoms off with a knife.

▼ Two glasses to fit under the bottles.

▼ Two cardboard tubes to slip over the bottles. They should fit snugly so that when you squeeze gently you can pick the bottle up with the tube (or do it by putting a finger in the top of the bottle).

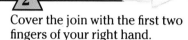

Glass and bottle under here.

1
Start with one glass under a bottle and a tube (A) and the second glass under the other bottle, next to the tube (B).

2
Lift up tube A and the bottle to show a glass. Slip tube B over the second bottle. Say you will swap the glass and bottle.

3
Look into both tubes and say that they have swapped. Now say that you will do the hard bit and make them swap back again.

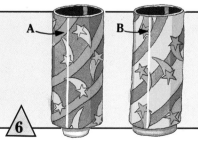

4
Lift tube A and bottle and tube B alone to show the bottle and glass where they were before. No-one will be impressed.

5
Say that as they don't believe you, you will do it again. Lift tube A to show a bottle and tube B and bottle to show a glass.

6
Make them swap back again by lifting tube B on its own and tube A and bottle. Make them swap back and forth quite fast.

Bangle on a String

For this trick you need a large ring (a plastic bangle is ideal), 6ft of string and a scarf.

First let spectators look at the ring and string. Don't give them the string for long. Pretend not to want it examined closely, to misdirect suspicion.

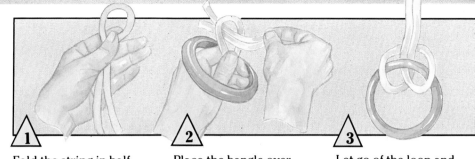

1 Fold the string in half and take hold of it near the loop that is made, as shown.

2 Place the bangle over the loop. Pick up the two loose ends of the string and thread them through the loop.

3 Let go of the loop and pull the ends. This knot will keep the bangle tightly fastened to the string.

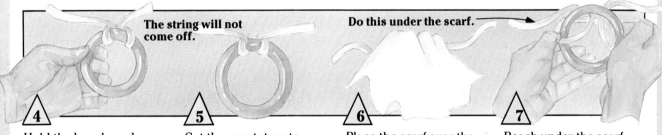

The string will not come off.

Do this under the scarf.

4 Hold the bangle and hand the string ends to two spectators. Ask them to try to pull the string off.

5 Get the spectators to stand on either side of you and pull hard on the string. The bangle remains firmly fixed.

6 Place the scarf over the bangle. Get the helpers to move a bit nearer to you to give you some slack string.

7 Reach under the scarf and slip the loops of the knot round and off the bangle, as shown. Whisk off the scarf.

Pegasus Coin

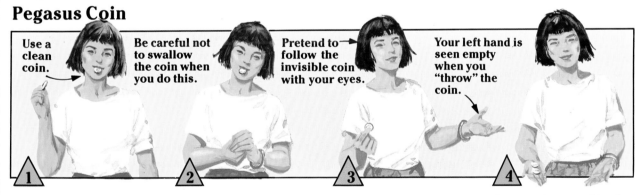

Use a clean coin.

Be careful not to swallow the coin when you do this.

Pretend to follow the invisible coin with your eyes.

Your left hand is seen empty when you "throw" the coin.

1 Show the audience a coin in each of your hands. Place the coin in your left hand between your lips.

2 Pretend to put the coin in your right hand into your left, but actually French Drop it to leave it in the right hand.

3 Take the coin from your lips with your right fingers. Mime throwing a coin from your left hand into the air.

4 As you mime catching it, drop the coin in your fingers on the one already in your hand and show both.

Variations to try

Thumb Surprise
1. Quick close-up trick.
2. Comedy for children.
3. "Pretend" loosening-up exercise before a trick.

Glasses and Bottles
1. Done silently.
2. Done with patter.
3. Played "straight".
4. Played for laughs.

Bangle on a String
1. Use ring, string and hankie in close-up.
2. Use hoop, rope and coat for cabaret.
3. In escapology act.

Pegasus Coin
1. Close-up trick.
2. Use as quick effect in cabaret, before the Miser's Dream (page 42), for example.

SNAPSHOTS FROM THE LIFE OF HOUDINI

Harry Houdini is probably still the most famous magician in the world, although he died over 60 years ago. He was born in 1874 and died on 31 October 1926. He was most famous as an escapologist, freeing himself from all sorts of seemingly impossible situations.

The Master Escapologist

His longest-running stage trick was called Metamorphosis. Inside a sack, with his hands tied, he was locked in a roped trunk.

His wife, Bess, drew a curtain in front of the trunk. Then she went behind the curtain and clapped her hands three times.

At the third clap, the curtains opened, and Houdini stepped out. Bess was in the sack in the trunk, tied as he had been.

Jail breaks

Houdini escaped from local jails for publicity. One of his most famous jail breaks was in Washington D.C.

He was locked naked in the cell which had held a famous assassin. His clothes were locked in another cell. He freed himself, moved the prisoners in the block around and found his clothes in under half an hour.

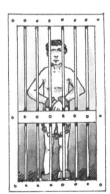

The Handcuff King

In England, he was challenged by a newspaper to escape from a pair of handcuffs which a locksmith had spent five years making. It took him 70 minutes to free himself.

The Water Can

Houdini was handcuffed and put in a big metal can, full of water. The lid was locked on. In three minutes, he was out, and the can was still locked.

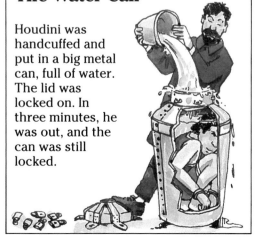

The Chinese Water Torture Cell

This was probably his most famous and spectacular escape. First his legs were trapped in stocks, which were part of the square lid of the "cell".

Then he was lowered upside-down into the "cell", which was a glass-fronted mahogany tank full of water. From this, too, he escaped in a few minutes.

Straitjackets

He often performed straitjacket escapes, and in 1914 he introduced a new twist to this stunt. He even escaped while dangling by his feet from a crane on top of a high building.

Battle against the mediums

A medium is someone who claims to communicate with the spirits of the dead. Houdini said such powers did not exist, and worked hard to expose fake mediums.

Investigating the claims of mediums, Houdini devised a box like this. It prevented mediums from using their feet to produce fake spirit effects.

He ended up showing the mediums' tricks as part of his act on stage. One example was ringing a bell with his foot, although both his feet were apparently controlled by an observer.

Safety first

Surprisingly, this was Houdini's motto. His escapes all had built-in safety precautions. He had also rigorously trained himself so he could safely do things it would be very dangerous for ordinary people to try. In fact, two people drowned copying his escapes.

Flying high

In 1910, Houdini tried out the Voisin biplane which he had bought in Germany. At 5 am on March 16th, he made the first successful flight in Australia.

Houdini in Hollywood

Houdini made some films in Hollywood, featuring spectacular escapes. He did most of the stunts himself. In one of the most hair-raising, he rescued a woman from a canoe on the brink of Niagara Falls.

The end of the story

Houndini died of appendicitis, caused by being hit in the stomach. He refused to cancel his show in spite of the pain, and when he got to hospital, it was too late. The anniversary of his death is now National Magic Day in America, when magicians follow Houdini by doing free shows in hospitals and children's homes.

STRING TRICKS

Magic Knot

In this trick, you seem to make a knot appear on a string just by flicking it in the air. To prepare, tie a simple knot near one end of a piece of string about 1m (1 yard) long.

1 Hold the string with the knot hidden behind your fingers. The unknotted end hangs down from your hand.

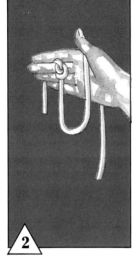

2 Flick the end of the string up and catch it between your thumb and first finger. Release it to hang as before.

3 Repeat step 2, then flick it again. This time, keep hold of this end and release the knotted one. A knot appears.

Mug Bet

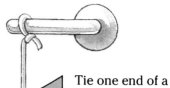

1 Tie one end of a piece of string to the handle of a mug and the other end to a door handle. Bet a friend that you can cut the string without the mug falling.

2 Tie a loop in the string and cut the loop. The mug is still hanging although the string is cut.

Threading the Needle

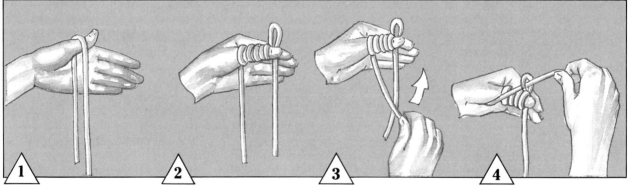

1 Hold a piece of string about 1m (1 yard) long so that about 15cm (6in) is hanging down between your thumb and your palm. Take hold of the other end of the string.

2 Wrap the string around your thumb several times and then form a loop with the end. Hold the loop against your first finger with your thumb.

3 Tell the audience that the loop represents the eye of a needle which you will thread impossibly quickly. Take hold of the other end of the string.

4 Sharply pull this end up between your thumb and forefinger, without parting them. Pull the string out slowly to show that the "needle" is threaded.

MORE MAGIC TRICKS

CONTENTS

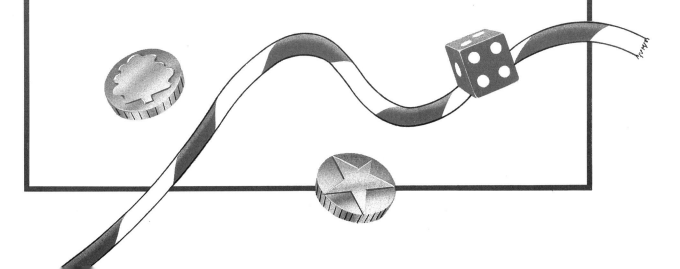

TRICKS FOR EVERYONE

This part of the book contains close-up tricks only. They are all designed to be performed to small audiences, or even only one or two people at a time. For more close-up tricks and techniques, see pages 30-39.

Choosing your tricks

As they are all close-up effects, the tricks in this part of the book are divided up according to what props they use. This means the tricks which are together may be quite similar. Try to put together tricks from different pages to make up your act.

Getting it right

Never forget how important it is to practise. Even when you know a trick really well, you can always improve on it. Remember to practise in front of a mirror whenever you can, and to ask friends to watch you and criticize your performance.

Where to find props

You can make props for some tricks, and others are cheap to buy. You may need to borrow the rest, so make sure you ask first and always be very careful with borrowed props.

Try to look different

You can dress how you like to do magic. A good way of getting clothes quite cheaply is going to junk shops and flea-markets. You may find some unusual bargains.

The right time

Although almost everyone likes magic tricks, they may not always want to watch them. Be aware of your audience and try to judge carefully whether it is a good time to show them some tricks.

Keep your audience interested

When you are making up an act, try to use a variety of props. Although some magicians specialize in magic with cards or coins, it may be best for you to keep it varied at first, to avoid boring your audience.

What you need

Like the tricks earlier in the book, these close-up effects use props which are easy to come by and cheap to buy. This case contains some of the things you can use for close-up magic.

Use bright new coins rather than older ones. They always look good and attract people's attention.

Playing cards come in lots of different colours and styles. New cards are easiest to handle, as they are quite slippery.

Looking after your props

If you use a lot of props, make sure you know where everything is. Your audience will get bored watching you search for a prop before each trick.

Where to perform

Close-up tricks are the most versatile kind of magic. You can do a trick or two wherever you like, as long as you have the right props.

Keep it a secret

Remember not to tell anyone how your tricks are done unless they are also real magic enthusiasts. Magicians don't reveal their secrets to anyone except fellow magicians.

MAGIC SKILLS

These two pages give reminders of useful magic expressions and techniques from earlier in the book, as well as Magician's Choice, which is only explained here. Find the Card is a trick which uses all of them. You could learn it to help you practise these techniques, especially the Magician's Choice bit at the end.

Face-up, face-down

The instructions for card tricks often tell you to deal cards "face-up" or "face-down". This is because a card has a "face", which shows its suit and value, and a back which is patterned and looks the same as the other cards in the pack.

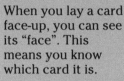

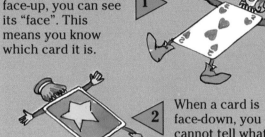

When you lay a card face-up, you can see its "face". This means you know which card it is.

When a card is face-down, you cannot tell what it is. You can only see its back.

Cutting cards

When you let volunteers cut the pack you must make sure they cut it this way. Otherwise the sequence of the cards is changed. You could cut the pack once yourself to show a spectator what to do.

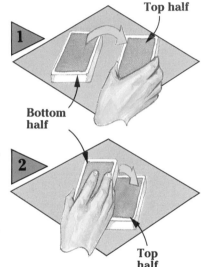

Take hold of the top of the pack and lift off roughly half.

Top half

Bottom half

Put this half face-down on the table and then complete the cut by putting the other half on top.

Top half

Misdirection

Whenever you are doing a magic trick, you need to be able to misdirect. This means you subtly direct your audience's attention away from what you are doing. Here are some reminders of basic ways of misdirecting. For more on misdirection, see pages 10-11.

Your eyes tell people where to look, so only look at what you want them to notice.

If you want people to think something is in your left hand when it is in your right, watch your left hand with interest and pay no attention to your right hand.

Do every move at the same speed. Changes of pace can make people suspicious.

Repeat a move a few times before doing a sleight (secret move) as part of it. People will not be watching so closely.

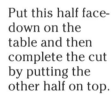

When you speak, people look at your face. Talk when you want to divert their attention away from your hands.

Your audience will be suspicious if they see you do something without a good reason. Make sure there is a reason for everything you do. For example, in step 1 of Find the Card when you want to Glimpse the bottom card of the pack, shuffle the cards first. This gives you a reason to square (tidy) the pack and do the Glimpse.

Magician's Choice

This is a useful magic technique which is used in Crosses Across, Double Six and One in Three.* You appear to let your volunteers choose quite freely, but you actually manipulate what they do so they "choose" the one you want them to have.

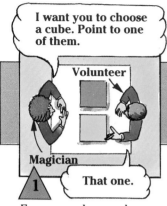

1 "I want you to choose a cube. Point to one of them." — "That one."

2 "That means you want that one." — "Yes, that's right."

3 "I want you to choose a cube. Point to one of them." — "That one."

4 "So that rules this one out." — "All right."

For example, you have two cubes, one red and one yellow, and you want a volunteer to choose the yellow one. You ask her to point to one.

If she points to the yellow cube, you take the red one away, leaving her with the yellow one, "because she has chosen the yellow one".

Your volunteer is just as likely to point to the one you don't want her to choose. If she does, stay calm and confident, and don't hesitate.

Tell her that she has ruled out the red cube, and take it away. Whichever she points to, you interpret her action to give the result you want.

You can vary this technique to cope with any choice. In One in Three, it is a choice between three things. You will need to do it twice unless your volunteer chooses correctly the first time. If you are brisk and confident, no-one will think of arguing with you.

Find the Card

This is an easy card trick which uses the techniques explained on these two pages. Squaring a pack of cards means tapping the edges on the table to tidy it up after shuffling it, and Glimpsing a card means looking at it quickly without anyone noticing.

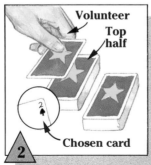

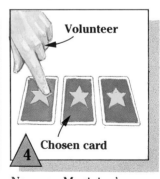

1 Shuffle the pack, then square it up like this and Glimpse the bottom card. Ask a volunteer to take a card from the pack and memorize it.

2 Now cut the pack and ask him to put his card on the top half. Complete the cut, then cut the pack a few more times, saying you are losing his card.

3 Look through the pack and take the card you Glimpsed and the two on its right. Put them face-down in the same order, saying you think one is his card.

4 Now use Magician's Choice to make the volunteer choose the middle card. Turn it over, thanking him for choosing the same card twice.

* Crosses Across is on p102, Double Six p92, and One in Three p111.

QUICK TRICKS

All these tricks are quite easy to do and fun to watch. Learn them so that you can do a quick trick whenever you have the right props with you.

Clever Clips

This is a fun way to link two paper clips, using a bank note.* Try changing the positions of the clips, and how sharply you pull, to see how the trick works best.

1 Fold a bank note a third of the way across, then clip the folded third to the rest of the note.

2 Fold the last third of the bank note behind the two thirds you have already clipped together.

3 Clip the last third to the middle layer, with the larger part of the paper clip inside the fold.

4 Hold the ends of the bank note and pull them firmly apart. The paper clips will jump off, linked together.

Cork Twist

This trick sounds quite hard, but with a bit of practice, you will find it really easy. Challenge your friends to do it. They will find it is harder than it looks.

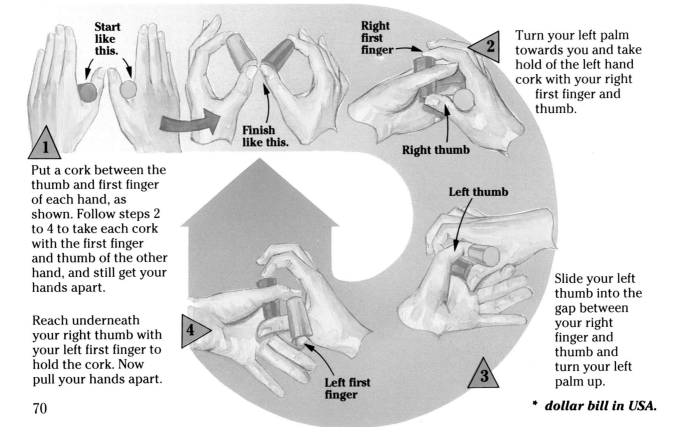

Start like this.

Finish like this.

1 Put a cork between the thumb and first finger of each hand, as shown. Follow steps 2 to 4 to take each cork with the first finger and thumb of the other hand, and still get your hands apart.

Reach underneath your right thumb with your left first finger to hold the cork. Now pull your hands apart.

Right first finger

Right thumb

2 Turn your left palm towards you and take hold of the left hand cork with your right first finger and thumb.

Left thumb

3 Slide your left thumb into the gap between your right finger and thumb and turn your left palm up.

4

Left first finger

70

* *dollar bill in USA.*

Vanishing Change

Take some coins from your pocket with your right hand and show them. Say you will make one of them vanish.

Pretend to take a coin with your left hand. Cup your right hand so the audience cannot see your left fingers.

Put the coins back into your pocket, and show the audience that your right hand is empty.

Pretend to put the coin in your right hand and close it. Turn it over and tap the back with your left hand.

Open your right hand to show that it is empty, and your left hand too. The coin has disappeared.

Sixes and Sevens

Take all the sixes and sevens out of a pack of cards. Arrange the sixes and the sevens like this. Do it openly, but do not draw attention to the order you are putting the cards in.

Ask a volunteer to cut the eight cards a few times. Most people do not know that this will not change the order of the cards. Take them back and say you can feel which ones are from each suit.

To prove it, take the eight cards behind your back. Hold them all in your right hand: the first four between your thumb and first finger, and the others between your first and second fingers.

With your left hand, take the top card of each set of four and drop them face-up on the table. Repeat this with the remaining cards, each time taking the top card from each set.

Take a while to make each pair. The trick will seem harder, and more impressive.

Newspaper Stand

How can two people stand on the same sheet of newspaper and not be able to touch each other?

Put the paper under a door and stand on either side of it.

EVEN QUICKER TRICKS

Squaring the Matches

Set up four matches exactly like this on the table-top. Challenge a friend to make a square by moving only one match.

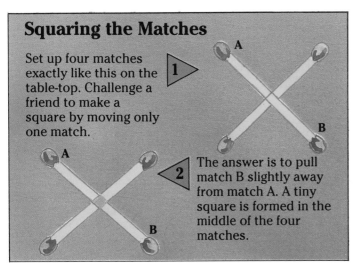

The answer is to pull match B slightly away from match A. A tiny square is formed in the middle of the four matches.

Lift the Bottle

How can you pick up an empty bottle with a drinking straw? This works best with a glass bottle, but make sure you have a hand underneath just in case it falls.

Bend the straw about two-thirds of the way up, and push the bent part into the bottle. It should wedge itself against the side of the bottle, letting you pick it up.

Vanishing Square

This prop is all you need for this trick. First draw a rectangle and 13 evenly-spaced squares in pencil on a piece of cardboard, like this. Then go over them in ink.

Cut out the rectangle, then cut along the red lines dividing A, B and C. Erase the pencil marks. Now you can start the trick.

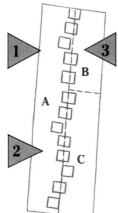

Place the pieces on the table like this. Ask a volunteer to count the squares. There are 13.

Rearrange the pieces, swapping C and B. Ask the volunteer to count again. This time there are only 12 squares. One has vanished.

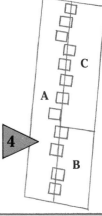

Making an Entrance

This is a silly joke which you can use when coming into a room. It works best with a door which opens away from you.

Pop your head around the door and say "Hello", holding the edge of the door with one hand.

Now reach behind your head with the other hand. Grab your neck and pull yourself back behind the door, acting surprised.

Pull the Cork

Push a tight-fitting cork into the neck of a plastic bottle. Then push it right inside. How can you get it out without breaking the bottle?

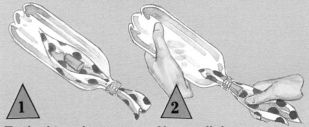

To do this, take a handkerchief or a thin tea-towel and push one end inside the bottle. Shake it so the cork falls against the handkerchief.

Now pull the handkerchief slowly out of the bottle. It should pull the cork out, too. It might be a bit stiff at the end, but keep pulling.

ROLL THE DICE

Dice Roll

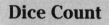

Magician's sum
6 + 5 + 4 + 7 = 22

Turned over

Rolled again

1 2 + 6 + 5 = 13

Turn your back, asking a friend to roll three dice and add up the numbers on them.

2 13 + 5 = 18

Ask him to turn one of the dice upside-down and add its new number to his total.

3 18 + 4 = 22

Now ask him to roll this dice again and add this third number to the total.

4

Turn back and silently add up the dice. Add seven to get your friend's total.

Three Dice Trick

This trick looks impressive and people will be unable to copy it. You need to moisten your first

finger and thumb before you start. Make sure no-one sees you do this.

1 Hold three dice between your thumb and first finger, like this. Release the pressure on the dice a little.

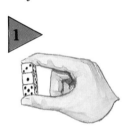

2 This lets the middle dice fall while the other two stay between your fingers, as they will stick to them slightly.

Tower of Dice

 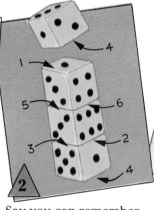 

Volunteer's sum:
4 + 1 = 5
+6 = 11
+5 = 16
+2 = 18
+3 = 21
+4 = 25
Magician's sum:
28 - 3 = 25

1 Turn your back, asking a volunteer to make a tower by putting four dice on top of each other, with the numbers in any position. Turn, glance at the top dice, and turn your back again.

2 Say you can remember some of the numbers you saw, and ask her to add up the numbers on the faces you did not see: the bottom of the top dice and the top and bottom of the other three.

3 Turn back and announce the total of the hidden faces: you will be right if you subtract the number on the top dice from 28, as the opposite faces of a dice always add up to 7.

Dice Count

2 × 2 = 4
4 + 5 = 9
9 × 5 = 45

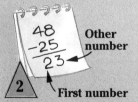

1 45 + 3 = 48

With your back turned so you cannot see the dice, ask someone to roll two dice and double the number on one of them. Then he should add five, multiply the answer by five, and add the number on the other dice.

48
−25
23

Other number

First number

2 Ask the volunteer his total. Subtract 25 from it. You will get a two-figure number, made up of the two numbers he rolled, first the one he used first and then the other.

MONEY MAGIC

Static Trick

Take a fairly thick coin and balance it on its edge. Now balance a match across the top of the coin. How can you move the match off the coin without touching either of them?

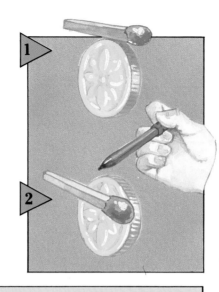

Rub a plastic pen on your hair or something made of nylon. Hold the pen close to the match. The static electricity on the pen makes the match move and fall off the coin.

Three Coin Trick

Put three coins in a row, with the middle one closer to the coin on one side than the other. Set them up slowly and carefully. Which coins are furthest apart? A lot of people will say A and B, but the answer is really A and C.

Double Your Money

Show a bank note, saying that you can double it. Fold it in half, and show it "doubled". The audience should groan.

Wait a second, then say seriously that you can really increase it. Fold it twice more, unfold it and show it to them "in creases".

Coin Circle

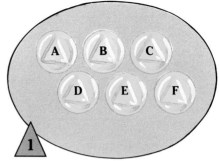

How can you move these coins to make a circle? You are only allowed three moves, and each coin you move must end up between two other coins.

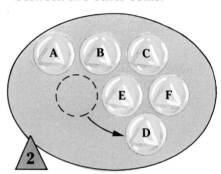

First move D between E and F.

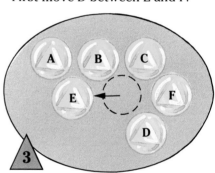

Then move E between A and B.

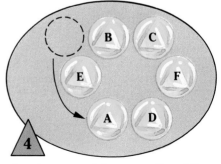

Lastly, move A between E and D.

Coin Hit

Put three coins touching each other in a row. How can you move coin A away from coins B and C? You are allowed to move but not touch coin A, touch but not move coin B, and touch and move C.

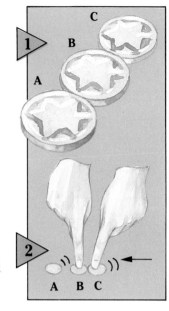

Hold B down with a finger, and knock coin C against B. Coin A will move away from B.

Catch it if You Can

Hold a bank note like this. Ask a volunteer to position his hand halfway down the note, ready to catch it when you drop it. Bet him he cannot catch it before it hits the ground. Almost no-one will be quick enough.

Volunteer's hand must not be touching the note.

Magician

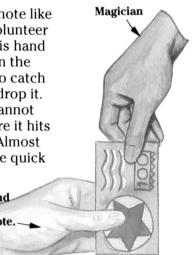

Four in a Row

Make an L-shape with six coins, four down and three across. How can you move one coin so that both rows have four coins in them?

Put coin A on top of coin B.

One Note or Two

These instructions tell you how to fold a bank note so that it looks like two. You could use it to joke about how rich you are, or to trick your friends.

1 Fold the bank note in half lengthways away from you, and cut a slit about 2.5cm (1in) long in the middle of the fold.

Cut a 2.5cm (1in) slit here.

2 Now unfold the note and fold it in half widthways, without turning it over.

3 Unfold it again and make a diagonal fold towards you from one end of the slit to about 2.5cm (1in) from the end of the note.

Diagonal fold

2.5cm (1in)

4 Then make another fold like this from the other end of the slit to the other long edge of the note.

2.5cm (1in)   **Diagonal fold**

5 Folding the note along the lengthways crease, take hold of both short ends of the note and push them towards the middle.

Push

Push

6 Now fold the note in half along the diagonal creases. It will look like two notes when you hold it up like this.

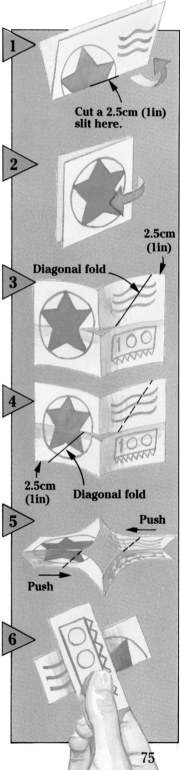

SELF-WORKING CARD TRICKS

Self-working tricks rely on certain cards being in certain positions in the pack. You need to set them up before you start, so your audience doesn't suspect anything.

Remember not to shuffle the cards by accident. Although these tricks are not difficult, they are really effective when performed smoothly.

Rising Cards

In this trick, you put two cards in the middle of a pack, and make them appear to rise to the top. To prepare, put the seven of hearts and eight of clubs on top of the pack.

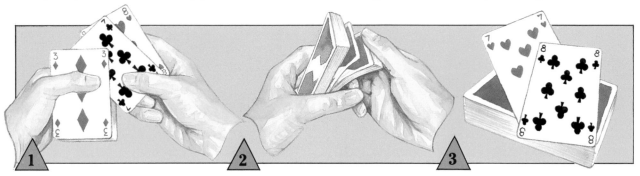

1 Take the seven of clubs and eight of hearts from the pack, pretending to choose then at random. Show them briefly to the audience, without naming them. Then put them into the middle of the pack.

2 Riffle the edges of the pack with your fingers, saying this will help the chosen cards rise to the top. Then put the cards down and tap the top of the pack, saying the cards should have arrived.

3 Turn over the top two cards: the seven of hearts and eight of clubs. These are not the cards you chose, but as you did not name them and they look very similar, the audience will not notice the difference.

Matching Pairs

Here you predict when a volunteer will tell you to stop dealing. Have the nine of clubs on top of the pack and the three of diamonds on the bottom.

1 Say you will pick two cards to match the ones he chooses when he stops you dealing. Take the three of hearts and nine of spades. Lay them face-down, without showing them.

2 Start dealing the cards face-down, asking your volunteer to say "Stop". When he does, lay the three of hearts face-up on the dealt cards, and put the rest of the pack on top of the three of hearts.

3 Now start dealing from the top of the pack again, asking the volunteer when to stop. This time put the nine of spades face-up on top of the dealt cards and the rest of the pack on top again.

4 Remind the volunteer that you chose your cards before dealing. Take the three of hearts and nine of spades out of the pack with the card above each of them. Reveal the matching pairs.

Double Prediction

Start with the ace of spades, two of hearts, four of diamonds and eight of clubs in this order on top of the pack. By adding up the values of some or all of these cards you can equal the value of any card (king=13=1+4+8). Also, each of the four cards matches a suit.

1 Take the four cards off the pack and put them in your pocket, keeping them squared to hide how many you are taking. Tell a spectator you have predicted the card he will choose. Ask him to name it.

2 Take out the cards which make up the named card's value. To predict its suit, show the card of the same suit last, even if it is not needed for the value. The cards shown make up the king of clubs.

Finding the Fours

To prepare for this trick, put the four fours 10th, 20th, 30th and 40th in the pack.

Ask a volunteer for a number between 10 and 20. If he says 16, deal 16 cards face-down. Say "16 is 1 and 6. 1 and 6 is 7", and deal six cards back onto the pack. Leave the seventh face-down on the table beside the other cards.

2 Ask for another number between 10 and 20. If it is 12 this time, deal 12 cards face-down. Say "12 is 1 and 2, 1 and 2 is 3", and deal two cards back onto the pack. Put the third card face-down as before.

3 Repeat this process twice more. Remind your volunteer that he could have chosen any numbers between 10 and 20. Now turn over the four cards. They are all fours.

Weighing Cards

1 Give any 13 red and 13 black cards to someone to shuffle. Start dealing them face-down, counting silently. Ask the volunteer to say "Stop". When she does, you can tell how many more or less red cards you have than she has black cards.

2 If you stopped before the 13th card, subtract the number of cards you dealt from 13. You have that many more red cards than she has black. If you stopped after 13, subtract 13 from the number you dealt. You have that many less red cards than she has black.

3 While you are working out the answer in your head, pretend to weigh your cards, as if this is the trick. Give your answer and ask the volunteer to check whether you are right by counting the number of red and black cards in the two hands.

Sticky Sugar

For this trick you need two lumps of sugar, one of which has a smear of butter on one side. You could set up a bowl of sugar-lumps on the table with the buttered one ready in it so you would appear to be taking two lumps at random.

1 Hold one lump between the forefinger and thumb of each hand, with the buttered side hidden.

2 Rub one lump against your sleeve, saying you will stick them together with static electricity.

3 Turn the buttered lump around and stick the lumps together. Hold them up to show everyone.

4 To finish the trick, get rid of the evidence by eating both lumps of sugar.

Balancing Grape

1 Start with your first finger pointing upwards, secretly holding a cocktail stick* behind it with your thumb. Keep the point just below the tip of your finger.

2 Tell the audience that you will balance a grape on your finger. Push the grape onto the cocktail stick, pretending to position it on the end of your finger.

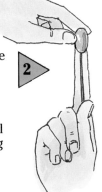

3 Move your hand as if it is difficult to keep the grape balanced, and pretend to concentrate hard. Keep your palm towards you to hide the cocktail stick.

4 To finish, take the grape off the cocktail stick and give it to someone in the audience to try the trick. While no-one is watching, put the stick in your pocket.

Take a Bite

1 Hold a coin between your first and second fingers, like this, and have a piece you have bitten off a white mint in your mouth.

2 Pick up a white mug in the same hand. Hold the coin squeezed between your fingers and the mug, but resting against your first finger. No-one should see the coin.

*** You could use a toothpick instead.**

Bouncing Apple

You need to be sitting at a table facing sideways to do this, so it is a good dinner-time trick. If you time the actions properly, as well as stamping your foot, it looks and sounds as if you really have bounced the apple on the floor.

1 Hold an apple in your hand and pretend to throw it at the floor, moving your arm below the table top. Try it with a ball to get the move right.

Stamp your foot.

2 As the apple goes below the table top, stamp your foot. Toss the apple into the air at once, still keeping your hand below the table top.

3 Bring your hand above the table to catch the apple as it falls again. A good finishing touch is to prove it is a real apple by biting it.

Raise the mug to your mouth. Press your second finger hard against the mug and lift your first finger slightly. The coin will slide off your finger and clink.

3 Coin clinks on mug.

Pull the mug away and spit out the piece of mint, looking astonished. Keep the mug tilted towards you or people will see you have not taken a bite out of it.

4

Now worriedly rub the rim of the mug with your other hand. Look relieved and tilt the mug away from you to show you have "mended" it.

5

Slicing a Banana

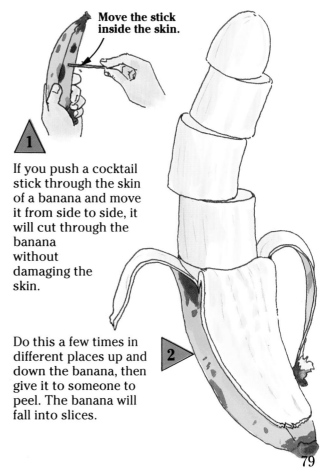

Move the stick inside the skin.

1 If you push a cocktail stick through the skin of a banana and move it from side to side, it will cut through the banana without damaging the skin.

2 Do this a few times in different places up and down the banana, then give it to someone to peel. The banana will fall into slices.

MAGIC WITH MATCHES

Magic Matchbox

Take the tray out of a box of matches and cut a piece off the end, about three-quarters of the way along.

Put the pieces of tray back into the cover, and mark the long end to recognize it. Put the matches back in, with their heads at the marked end.

To start the trick, hold the box upright. Push the unmarked end a little and pull out the long end of the tray. It looks as if the matchbox is empty.

Push in the marked end, then open the box again by pushing on the short end. The matches have appeared in the box.

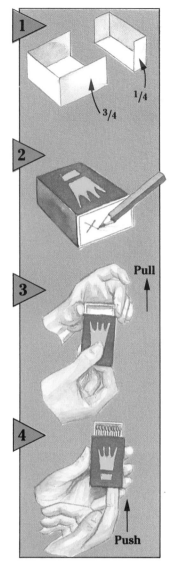

Tip

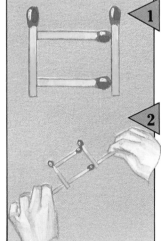

Keep the Magic Matchbox in a special place, or you might try to use it for another trick. This could ruin that trick as well as giving away the secret of Magic Matchbox. Always make sure you know where your props are.

Matchbox Challenge

This stunt is difficult, but if you practise a lot, it will become easier. Then you can challenge your friends, and they will find it much harder than it looks.

Empty the tray of a matchbox and stand it on one end. Lay the cover down in front of the tray.

Resting the tips of your second and third fingers on the table, grip the tray between your first and little fingers.

Keeping your second and third fingers on the table, lift the cover and put it on top of the tray.

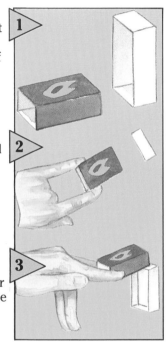

Lift the Matches

Set up four matches on the table as in the picture. How can you lift them all off the table, using two other matches?

Press the two matches against the uprights, exactly opposite the ends of one of the cross-bars. Start lifting them slowly and carefully off the table. It will work when you get the positions exactly right.

Be careful not to strike a match by accident when you are doing any of these tricks.

Escaping Match

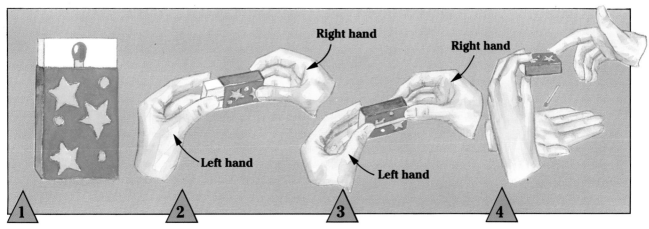

1 Before you start, slide a match between the cover of a full matchbox and the bottom of the tray. Make sure this match faces the same way as the matches in the box.

2 In front of the audience, open the box and remove the cover with your right hand. Keep hold of the tray and the match underneath it with your left hand.

3 Carefully replace the cover, holding the end of the match with your left thumb. Make sure the match stays outside the cover, and hold it there with your thumb.

4 Hold the box over a friend's hand and give it a tap. Let the match drop into her hand. It looks as if it has escaped through the bottom of the matchbox.

Match Glass Puzzle

Make a glass shape from four matches, like this. Put a small coin in the "glass". How can you move the "glass" so the coin is outside it? You can only move two matches.

1

2 Slide match C to the left so that match A is halfway along it.

3 Then move match B to the left-hand end of match C.

Pyramid of Matches

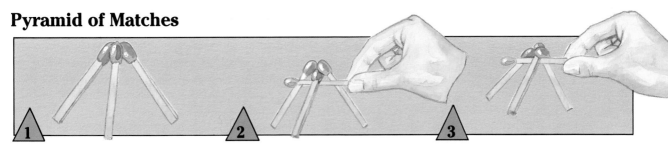

1 Glue two matches together by the ends and lean a third against them so they stand up like this. How can you lift the three matches off the table with another match?

2 Put the fourth match between the two stuck matches and the balanced one. Push the stuck matches slightly so that the balanced one falls between them onto the fourth match.

3 By lifting the fourth match you can trap the three matches together and lift them all off the table, still in the pyramid shape they formed standing on the table.

CARD DISCOVERIES

These are tricks where a volunteer chooses a card and replaces it in the pack. Then the magician finds the chosen card without having seen it.

Single Reverse

1 Ask a spectator to take a card and memorize it. Face away from him, saying you don't want to see the card. Turn the pack over and turn the top card upside-down, so the pack has two "tops".

2 Turn back, take the spectator's card and push it into the pack. Do it slowly, so the audience does not see the cards are upside-down. Say you are trying to memorize the card's position.

Cards behind back

3 Put your hands behind you, saying you will try to find the card. Turn the top card over again, and turn the pack over. Spread the cards face-down on the table. The spectator's card will be face-up.

Tip

Try to keep the cards squared when you do a Reverse trick. If someone sees the edge of a card's face, they may realize the cards are upside-down.

Double Reverse

This is a more complicated version of the Single Reverse. Ask a volunteer to shuffle the pack and give you roughly half. Ask him to look at a card from his half and put it face-down on the table. Say you will do the same, and turn your back.

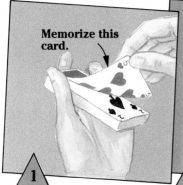

Memorize this card.

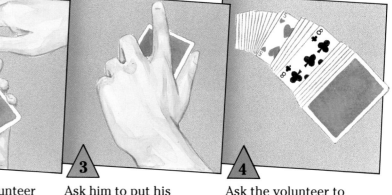

1 Turn your cards over, memorize the top card and turn it upside-down. Take another card and pretend to memorize it. Turn back and put it face-down on the table.

2 Now ask the volunteer to copy exactly what you do. Holding your cards as if you are about to deal them, slide his chosen card into them, without looking at it.

3 Ask him to put his cards on the table, pointing to a place with your left hand. Turn your hand as you point, reversing your cards again. Put them on top of his.

4 Ask the volunteer to name his card. Name the card you turned upside-down, and spread the pack face-down on the table. Your chosen cards will both be face-up.

The Card in Mind

In this trick, you find a card which a volunteer has not even taken from the pack. If you don't get the cards you need in step 1, ask the volunteer to shuffle the pack and deal again.

Memorize this card.

1 Ask a volunteer to deal you 15 cards. Take a spade, a heart, a diamond and two clubs, and show them arranged like this. Ask him to memorize one of the cards, remembering the last card yourself.

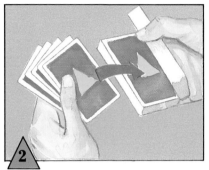

2 Put your five cards on the pack and the other ten on top of them. Now put the top five cards in the middle of the pack, then the bottom five, then the new top five. Your five cards are on top again.

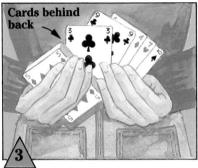

Cards behind back

3 Hold the pack behind you and ask the volunteer to name his chosen card. You know the last card of the top five and the order of the suits, so you can pick out his card. Produce the chosen card.

Last Card Left

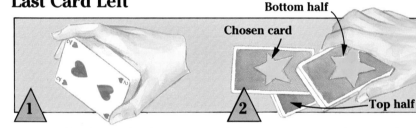

Bottom half

Chosen card

Top half

Glimpsed card on bottom

1 First shuffle the pack a few times. Then tap it on the table to square it up, turning the cards slightly towards you to Glimpse the bottom card.

2 Ask a spectator to take a card and memorize it. Cut the pack on the table. Ask him to lay his card on the top half. Then put the bottom half on top.

3 Have the pack cut a few times, then pick up the cards to look for his. When you find the card you Glimpsed, cut the pack so that it is on the bottom again.

Put 21 cards behind the others.

Chosen card

4 Say you cannot find his card. Look through the pack again, silently counting 21 cards. Put these cards on top of the pack, saying you will have to find his card another way.

5 Deal the pack face-down into two piles, dealing the first card to the spectator, then alternately. Ask him to look through his half of the pack for his card. He will not find it.

6 Deal your pile into two, dealing the first card to the spectator as before. Ask him to look again. Repeat this until you only have one card left. This card is the one he chose.

PAPER TRICKS

These tricks all involve cutting, tearing, or folding paper. You use a playing card for one and a postcard for another. Think before cutting things up, especially playing cards: use a joker or a card from a pack which is already incomplete.

Expanding Card

Take a playing card, or a piece of card the same size. Bet a friend that you can put your head through it. Fold it in half widthways and cut a slit, like this.

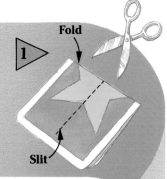

Fold

1

Slit

Unfold the card and cut short slits from the long edges towards the centre slit. If you cut through to the centre slit, you will need to start on a new card.

2

Short slits

Cut more short slits between the others, starting at the centre slit and cutting as close to the edges as possible.

3

Cut from centre slit.

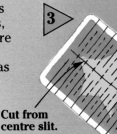

4 You can now open up a hole in the card big enough to put your head through. The more slits you cut, the bigger the hole will be.

Linking Card

Make this puzzle in secret so no-one sees how to do it. Unless you tear or cut something, you can only take the rings off the card by bending it as in step 4.

Cut two parallel slits lengthways down the middle of a postcard, about 1.25cm (0.5in) apart, leaving 2.5cm (1in) uncut at one end.

Now cut a hole in the 2.5cm (1in) space at the end of the card, slightly wider than the strip between the slits.

Cut two cardboard rings just too wide to fit through the hole. Tie them together with **a piece of string about 25cm (10in) long.**

Bend the card and pull the strip through the hole. Loop the rings onto the strip by **feeding the string through.**

Straighten the card again. It will look like this. Now you can challenge someone to take the rings and string off the card.

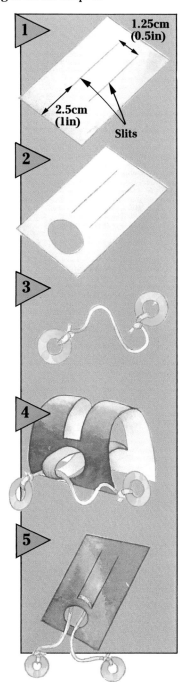

1 **1.25cm (0.5in)**

2.5cm (1in)

Slits

2

3

4

5

Make a Movie

Here is a way to make a simple moving picture. When you know how to do it, try other pictures.

10cm (4in)

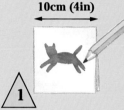

1

Cut a strip of paper 20cm by 10cm (8in by 4in). Fold it in half widthways and draw this picture on the top.

2

Draw this picture on the bottom flap, so that it lies right underneath the picture on the top flap.

3

Roll the top flap tightly around a pencil and hold the paper by the fold at the top. Move the pencil up and down to roll and unroll the top flap. The picture moves.

Paper Tree

1

Take a sheet of fairly thin coloured paper or newspaper and roll it up tightly, starting from one of the short sides. Hold one end with an elastic band.

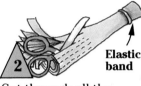

Elastic band

2

Cut through all the layers to about halfway down the roll. Do this in three or four places, always starting at the same end.

3

Take hold of the middle layer and pull it gently but firmly out of the roll. Don't worry if it tears. The tree will still look fine.

4

For a brown tree with green leaves, stick three sheets of green paper together with a brown one at the end. Roll them with the brown one outside.

Paper Tear

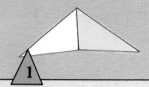

1

Tear a little triangle from the margin of a newspaper and fold it in half.

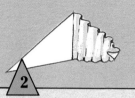

2

Crinkle one half of the triangle and fold it so that it stands out.

3

Moisten the flat half and stick it on the wallpaper. It will look like a tear.

4

Be careful who you try this joke on. Not everyone will be amused.

Instant Change

This is a very quick trick. The audience see you pass a small coin from one hand to the other, but as you do so, it seems to change into a much larger coin.

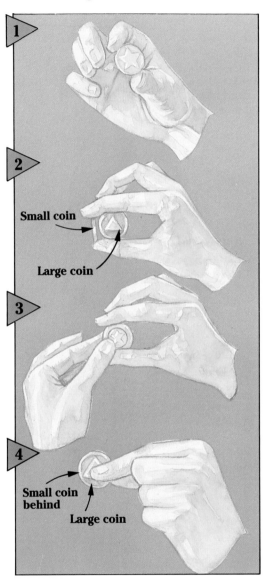

Hold a small coin by its rim between the thumb and first finger of your right hand.

Hold a larger coin behind the first, at right angles to it, so that the audience cannot see it behind the smaller coin.

Small coin

Large coin

Move your left hand over to take the coins. Your left thumb pushes the small coin so that it turns and is hidden beside the larger one.

Take the larger coin with the small one behind it between your left first finger and thumb and show it to the audience.

Small coin behind

Large coin

Hold a coin in your right hand and ask a volunteer to hold her hands out, palms up. Ask her to close her hands over the coin on the count of three.

Coin Optic

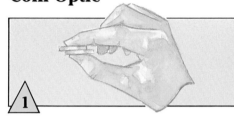

Hold two coins flat on top of each other between your thumb and forefinger like this, sideways to the audience. Say you will make an extra coin by rubbing them together.

Turning Coins

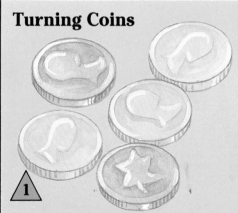

Throw some coins onto the table, and note silently whether there are an odd or even number of heads.

Tip

In tricks like Instant Change, coins can "talk", or clink when they are not supposed to. The only way to avoid this is to practise handling the coins smoothly.

2

Raise your hand above your head and bring it down to touch her hands with the coin. Count one. Do this again and count two as you touch her palms.

Coin on head

3

The third time you raise your hand above your head, leave the coin on top of your head. Then bring down your empty hand to hers, counting three.

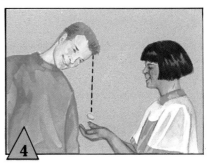

4

Show her the coin has gone, then say you will re-produce it if she keeps her hands still. Tilt your head forward. The coin will fall into her hands.

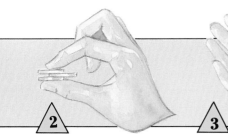

2

Rub the coins quickly backwards and forwards against each other. It looks as if there are three coins, not two.

3

Learn to do this with a coin squeezed between the fleshy base of your thumb and palm. This is called a Classic Palm.

4

Then if a spectator says it is only an optical illusion, you can throw three coins down onto the table.

Tip

It is easier to do this trick on someone who is shorter than you.

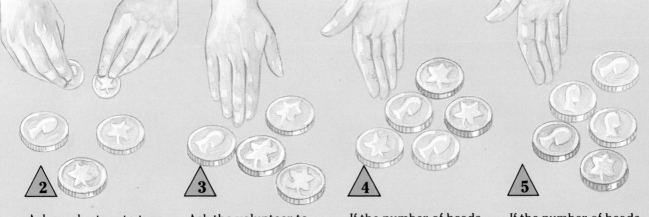

2

Ask a volunteer to turn the coins over as many times as she likes, but always two at a time, never singly. Turn your back.

3

Ask the volunteer to cover one coin. When you turn back, you can predict whether the hidden coin is a head or a tail.

4

If the number of heads was odd before and is still odd, or was even before and is still even, then the hidden coin is a tail.

5

If the number of heads was odd before and is now even, or was even before and is now odd, then the hidden coin is a head.

TRICKS WITH HANDKERCHIEFS

Knots and Crosses

Bet a friend that you can tie a knot in a handkerchief without letting go of the ends.

Stretch the handkerchief diagonally and lay it on the table in front of you.

Let go of the handkerchief and cross your arms. Now take hold of the ends of the handkerchief.

Slowly unfold your arms, still holding the ends of the handkerchief.

By unfolding your arms you transfer the "knot" in them to the handkerchief.

Funny Face

This is a good joke to do with glasses or sun-glasses. You could use it as an introduction to a series of tricks with handkerchiefs.

Lay a handkerchief over your face, and put on your glasses over the handkerchief. Put something in your mouth as well to make it look funnier.

Tip

Make sure your handkerchiefs are clean and ironed. Shabby props make you look like a bad magician even before you start.

Straight Through

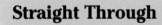

1 Make a circle by bending your left fingers to meet your thumb. Drape a handkerchief over this hand.

2 Push your right first finger down into the centre of the handkerchief, to make a well in it.

You are making a channel through the handkerchief.

3 Now secretly part your left fingers and thumb slightly and bring your middle finger in beside your first finger.

Loose Ends

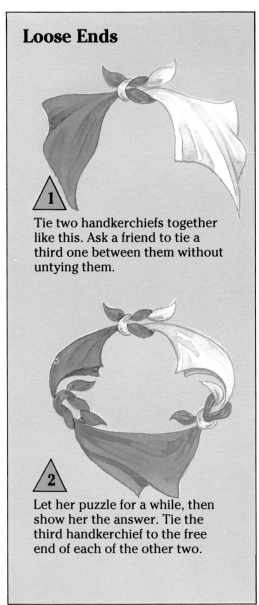

1 Tie two handkerchiefs together like this. Ask a friend to tie a third one between them without untying them.

2 Let her puzzle for a while, then show her the answer. Tie the third handkerchief to the free end of each of the other two.

1 Hold a handkerchief by the middle and pull it up through your right fist. Grip it between your right thumb and forefinger and curl the other fingers loosely around it.

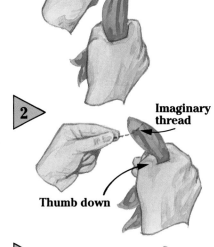

2 Pretend to tie a thread to the handkerchief, and to tug it with your left hand, moving your right thumb down the handkerchief a little. It moves as if it is being pulled.

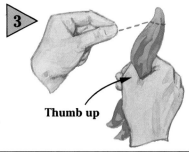

Imaginary thread

Thumb down

3 Bring your left hand a little closer to your right and move your thumb back up the handkerchief. It moves as if the thread has been slackened. Repeat a few times.

Thumb up

Tip

Think about what to do with your "invisible prop" at the end of the trick. It looks bad if you just forget it. Pretend to untie the thread or break it and throw it away.

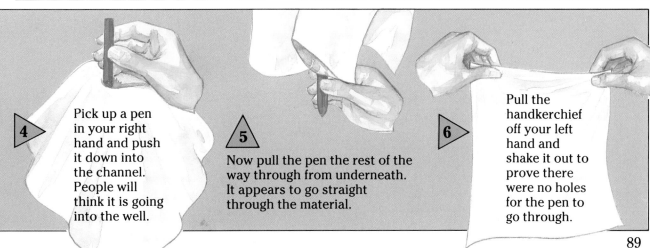

4 Pick up a pen in your right hand and push it down into the channel. People will think it is going into the well.

5 Now pull the pen the rest of the way through from underneath. It appears to go straight through the material.

6 Pull the handkerchief off your left hand and shake it out to prove there were no holes for the pen to go through.

Cheats and gamblers invented many of the techniques now used in card tricks, as ways of improving their chances of winning. The tricks below show the kinds of things gamblers did. You could present them as a demonstration.

Gambler's tip

Like a gambler playing cards, a magician must learn to control his expression. It is very important that his face should not tell people when he is up to something.

Dealing Fives

Say one way gamblers can improve their luck is by dealing themselves the cards they want.

Here you demonstrate this, dealing three fives to the audience every time you deal.

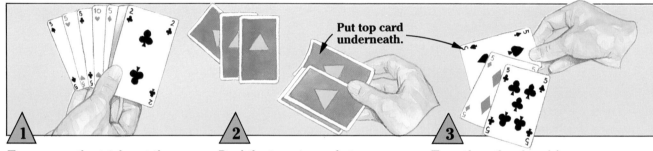

Put top card underneath.

1 To prepare the trick, set the pack up exactly like this, with a black five on top, then a red five, the other black five, any card and then the other red five.

2 Deal the top six cards to your audience and yourself in turn, starting with the audience. Put your top card under the other two and put all three cards back on the pack.

3 Turn the other hand face-up, then slide the top card under the other two. Show the audience that this hand contains one red five between two black fives.

Bottom and Centre Dealing

Here you show how cards can be dealt from the bottom of the pack, and then pretend to take others from the middle of the pack to get a winning hand. To prepare, secretly set up the pack with the two, three, four and five of spades on top.

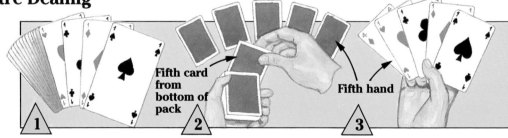

Fifth card from bottom of pack

Fifth hand

1 Openly put the four aces at the bottom of the pack, with the ace of spades right at the bottom. Say you will now demonstrate bottom dealing.

2 Start dealing five hands. Deal the first four cards normally, but the fifth from the bottom of the pack. Repeat this until each hand has five cards.

3 Turn the fifth hand over. It contains the four aces. Now put all the hands back on top of the pack, saying you will show off centre dealing.

Tip

Do not worry if your hands seem too small for the cards you are using. If you keep practising, you will overcome the problem.

4

Put the cards back on the pack and deal again. Even though you deal alternately to the audience and yourself, the same three cards seem to come back to the audience every time.

Many gamblers' tricks involve a lot of dealing. Try to keep things moving so you don't bore your audience.

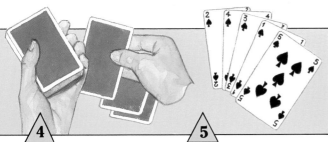

4

Deal another five hands of five cards. Deal suspiciously fast every time you come to the fifth hand, but actually deal all the cards normally.

5

Turn over the fifth hand again for a surprise ending. The audience may be expecting the four aces again, but it is the ace to five of spades.

Gambler's Bluff

A good gambler's voice will not give away his cards. Here you pretend to recognize a chosen card from the tone of a volunteer's voice. To prepare, put the four aces aside and secretly put six hearts on top of the pack and six on the bottom.

Volunteer

1

Ask a volunteer to deal the 48 cards into six piles, take a card from the middle of a pile and memorize it.

2

Then ask her to put her card on top of any pile, and put the other piles on top and underneath.

3

Let her cut the pack a few times, then ask her to deal the cards face-up, naming them as she deals them.

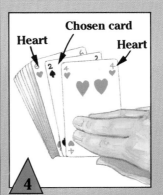

Heart   Chosen card   Heart

4

Stop her when you hear a card between two hearts. It is her card. Pretend you knew from her voice.

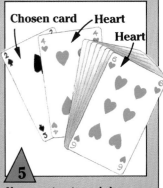

Chosen card   Heart   Heart

5

If you miss it, ask her to deal again. It could be the first card in the pack if the second is a single heart.

91

Pencil Twist

This is quite a difficult puzzle at first, but it soon becomes very easy. When you can do it easily, show it to your friends once and bet that they will not be able to do it.

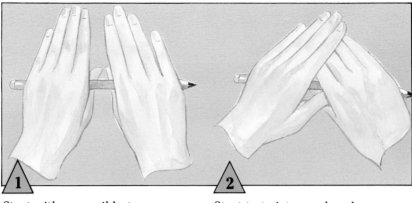

1 Start with a pencil between your thumbs and palms, like this. The puzzle is to move the pencil to on top of your hands without letting go.

2 Start to twist your hands, so that your right thumb goes under your left thumb, and your right fingers go under your left fingers.

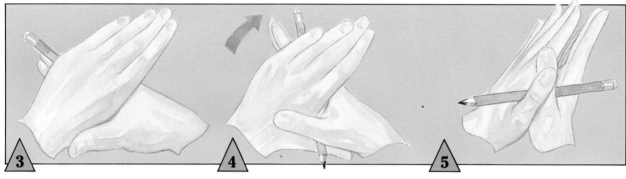

3 Twist your right hand down, so the base of your left thumb is between your right first finger and thumb, with the pencil across your left palm.

4 Now twist your right hand so that your first finger goes across your left palm and fingers, pushing the pencil upwards as it turns.

5 Twist your right hand until your palms are together. Now uncross your thumbs. The pencil is on top of your hands instead of underneath.

Double Six

6 has only one torn edge.

1 Cut a strip of paper and write the numbers 1-10 in ten equal sections on the strip. Make sure that 6 and 9 are at the ends, and the "9" is an upside-down 6.

2 Tear the paper into ten pieces, and make two face-down piles of five. Put the 6 in one pile and the "9" in the other. (They are the pieces with only one torn edge).

3 Take another piece of paper and write SIX on it, then fold it up and put it aside. Say you have predicted which number a volunteer will choose.

Pencil under here

Tip

Remember how important acting is. If you act surprised or pleased at your tricks, your audience will be pleased too.

You could do this trick indoors or under an umbrella. Firmly hold a piece of paper with a pencil underneath it, like this. Now move your thumb very slightly. It will make a sound like a raindrop falling.

Each time you move your thumb, look up for the drips, holding the paper as if to catch them. If you are good at bluffing, you can fool people that there is a leak.

Disappearing Pencil

1
Holding a coin in one hand, pick up a pencil in the other. Raise the pencil to beside your head, saying you will make the coin disappear.

2
Lower the pencil to tap the coin in an exaggerated magic gesture. Do this a few times, looking worried when the coin does not disappear.

3
Raise the pencil a last time and stick it behind your ear. Lower your hand to touch the coin, and look surprised that the pencil has gone.

4
After a time you can turn your head, revealing the pencil behind your ear. People will laugh when they see how they have been fooled.

Number 6

Volunteer

4
Ask your volunteer to choose one pile and destroy it. Divide the other pile into two, making sure the 6 is in the pile of two pieces.

5
Now ask her to touch a pile. Whichever it is, ask her to destroy the pile of three pieces.* Lay the last two face-down and ask her to pick up one of them.

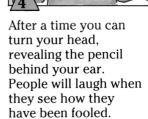

SIX

Magician

Volunteer

6
If she takes the 6, reveal your prediction. If she takes the other piece, tell her to destroy it. Then ask to see the last piece and reveal your prediction.

Use Magician's Choice to do this – see p69.

COIN JUGGLING

Hand Catch

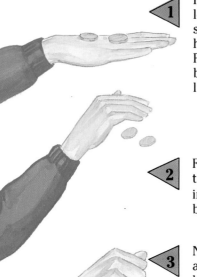

1 Hold your arm out, level with your shoulder, with your hand palm-down. Put two coins on the back of your hand, like this.

2 Flick your hand up, tossing the coins into the air. Quickly bend your arm.

3 Now straighten your arm, moving your hand forward to catch the coins before they fall.

Elbow Catch

Bend your arm so that your hand is resting palm-up on your shoulder. Balance a coin on your elbow. By straightening your arm very quickly, you should be able to catch the coin as it comes off your elbow. When you have practised a bit, you will be able to do it with more than one coin.

Balancing Coin

In this trick, you balance a coin on your right first finger. It appears to be attached to your finger as you slap it into the palm of your other hand and then bring it back again.

1 First show the audience a fairly large coin balanced on the end of your right first finger.

2 As you turn your hand to slap the coin down, hold the coin between your first finger and thumb, like this.

Hide the coin with your other fingers.

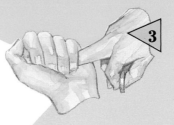

3 At the same time stretch out your right middle finger, and slap it down into your left palm.

4 Reverse the steps, and show the audience the coin still balanced on your right first finger.

Coin Roll

This is a very difficult flourish (an eye-catching effect), which needs lots of practice. Once you can do it quickly and confidently, it looks really impressive, as if the coin is tripping across your hand all on its own. Although you can do it with either hand, use the one you write with at first, as it will be your stronger hand.

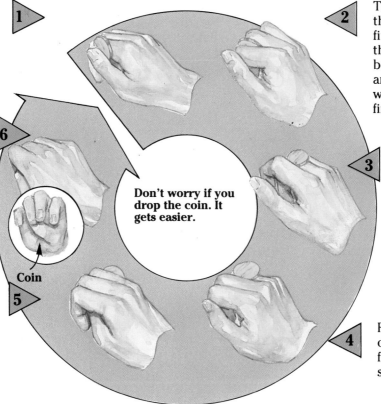

1 ▷ Hold a fairly large coin against the first joint of your first finger with your thumb, like this.

2 Tip the coin onto the back of your first finger with your thumb. Pull it between your first and second fingers with your second finger.

3 Now tip the coin onto the back of your second finger with your first finger.

4 Roll the coin over onto your third finger, using your second finger.

5 ▷ Now tip the coin into the gap between your third and little fingers. Bring your thumb across under your little finger and catch the coin as it slides down.

6 ▷ With your thumb, squeeze the coin flat underneath your fingers. Slide it back across and bring it up beside your first finger to start again.

Coin

Don't worry if you drop the coin. It gets easier.

Coin Roll Vanish

When you have mastered the Coin Roll and you can do it without thinking, try this. The effect is quite easy to do, and adds a magic emphasis to the flourish.

1 Do the Coin Roll steps 1-5, and when the coin slides down between your fingers, pretend to take it with your other hand. Curl your fingers to hide what you are doing.

Watch this hand.

2 Casually drop the hand with the coin to your side, hiding the coin. Put your empty hand in your pocket, watching it as you do it. Pretend to leave the coin in your pocket.

3 As this hand goes into your pocket, move the other hand forward, doing step 6 of the Coin Roll, and start the Roll again. It looks as if you have produced another coin.

ELASTIC BAND TRICKS

An elastic band is the only prop you need to do the tricks on these two pages. If you twist them cleverly, you can make elastic bands do surprising things.

Snap

This effect is hard to get right at first, but well worth the effort. In the trick, the audience hears you snap a band and sees the break, but you immediately mend it "by magic". Practise a lot until you can do steps 1-5 really quickly and easily.

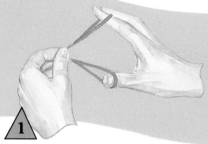

1 Loop the band around your right thumb and first finger. Take hold of the middle of the loop with your left thumb and first finger.

2 Pull your hands apart. Bring your right thumb and first finger together, letting the loop from your thumb slip onto your finger.

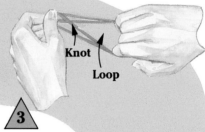

Knot

Loop

3 Put the rest of your fingers into the right hand side of the figure eight you have made. Stretch it around them so it looks like a single thickness.

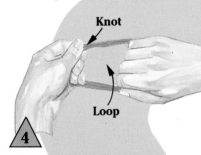

Knot

Loop

4 Now put your left fingers into the loop, taking hold of the knot between your left first finger and thumb. Keep the band stretched tightly.

5 Take your right first finger out of the loop. Then hold the band beside your left thumb and first finger with your right thumb and first finger.

6 Still keeping the double loop stretched to look like a single loop, pull your hands apart. The band will make a convincing snapping noise.

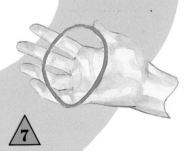

7 Show the "snapped" band for a moment, then gather it into your right hand. Blow into your hand and pull out the "mended" elastic band.

Through Your Thumb

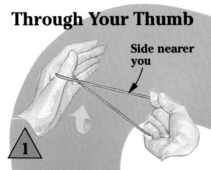

Side nearer you

1 Loop a band around your left thumb. Twist the band so that the side nearer to you goes over the other side.

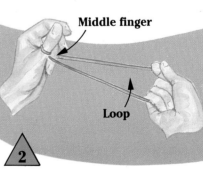

Middle finger

Loop

2 Put the middle finger of your left hand into the loop you have made by twisting the band.

Floating Band

This effect is hard to do fast, but when you can, the band seems to float off your fingers. Ask someone to copy you. It is not as simple as it looks.

1 Hold an elastic band around your two forefingers and twirl it around them.

2 Stop twirling and take the band between the forefinger and thumb of both hands.

3 Move your hands together until each thumb touches the opposite forefinger.

4 Now spread your fingers and thumbs and let the band fall onto the table.

Leaping Band

If you wrap a small band around your first two fingers in a certain way, you can make it jump from one finger to the other. This works even if someone holds the end of your first finger.

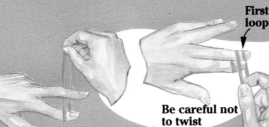

First loop

Be careful not to twist the band.

Volunteer

1 Put the band on the first finger of your left hand. With your right first finger and thumb, pull the band behind your left middle finger, like this.

2 Pull the band over your middle finger to loop onto your first finger again. Ask someone to hold your first finger to stop the band escaping.

3 Now bend your middle finger so that the first loop of the band comes off. The band will jump off your first finger onto your middle finger.

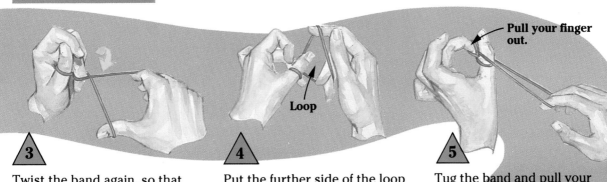

Loop

Pull your finger out.

3 Twist the band again, so that the side further from you comes over the other side of the band.

4 Put the further side of the loop over the top of your left thumb, without taking your middle finger out.

5 Tug the band and pull your middle finger out. The band seems to go straight through your thumb.

Piano Trick

You can do this trick with anything which will fit between someone's fingers, but playing cards are best. It is important to say things correctly so your volunteer comes to the right conclusion. You misdirect * by stressing that a pair is always an even number.

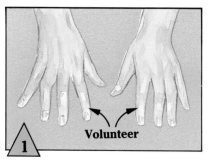

1 Volunteer

Ask a volunteer to put his hands palm-down on the table, with the fingers bent as if he were playing the piano.

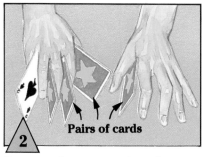

2 Pairs of cards

Start to place pairs of cards between each of his fingers, saying "A pair even" as you put each pair in place.

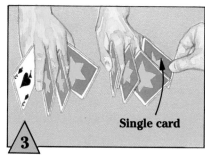

3 Single card

Place a single card between his last two fingers. Make sure the volunteer notices the single card. Say "One card – odd".

4 Magician

Remove the cards in the same order. Take each pair, saying "A pair – even" and divide it, making two piles of cards.

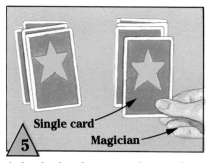

5 Single card / Magician

Ask which pile to put the single card on. Lay it down, saying "An even number plus an odd number is an odd number".

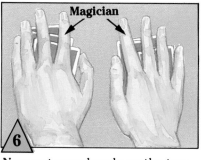

6 Magician

Now put your hands on the two piles of cards, saying you will make the single card move from the odd pile to the even one.

7 Volunteer

Ask the volunteer to count the cards in both piles. The odd pile will have eight cards (even) and the other will have seven (odd).

How it works

As you repeat that each pair is even, the volunteer will not realize that when you divide 7 pairs of cards, you make two piles of 7 (odd) cards. Adding the single card to one pile makes 8, which is even, not odd.

Eleven Fingers

Hold up your fingers in front of you and say you can prove you have 11 fingers. Count the fingers on one hand like this: "10, 9, 8, 7, 6", then look at the other hand and say "And 5 makes 11".

     See p10-11 for misdirection.

Front **Back**

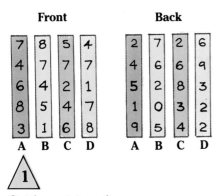

A	B	C	D	A	B	C	D
7	8	5	4	2	7	2	6
4	7	7	7	4	6	6	9
6	4	2	1	5	2	8	3
8	5	4	7	1	0	3	2
3	1	6	8	9	5	4	2

1

Cut four strips of paper or cardboard about 15cm (6in) long and 2.5cm (1in) wide. Write the sets of five numbers as shown in the picture on the front and back of the strips.

Volunteer's sum

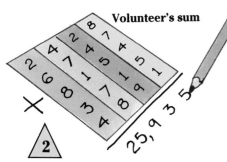

2

Ask a volunteer to mix the strips up and turn them over as much as he likes. Then he should line them up and add together the five four-figure numbers he had made, using a calculator or pen and paper.

$$\begin{array}{r} 3715 \\ 22220 \\ \hline 25,935 \end{array}$$

Magician's sum

3

While the volunteer is working it out, add the fourth four-figure number to 22220. You will get the same answer as the volunteer, but much faster than him. Amaze him by announcing it straight away.

Counting Sheep

This is a fun story with some silly sums in it. You could illustrate it with sheep made out of paper.

1

A man had a flock of 19 sheep. He wanted to give each of his three children a share: half to the eldest, a quarter to the middle one and a fifth to the youngest.

2

He realized that this plan would involve chopping up sheep. To avoid doing this, he borrowed an extra sheep from one of his friends. Now he had 20 sheep all together.

3

He gave 10 sheep (half) to the eldest, 5 (a quarter) to the middle one, and 4 (a fifth) to the youngest. Then he gave the sheep he had borrowed back to his friend.

How it works

19 is a prime number. It can only be divided by 1 and 19 – not 5, 4, or 2. To avoid chopping up sheep, the man needs a number which can be divided by 5, 4, and 2 – like 20. $1/5$, $1/4$, and $1/2$ only make $19/20$, not 1, so the farmer has one sheep left over to return to his friend.

Vanishing Grape

In this trick, you make a grape vanish and then reappear in your mouth. To do this, you use the French Drop (see p8.). You need to sit at a table to do this trick.

You need two grapes for the trick: one on the table, the other hidden in your right hand. You can hold it Finger Palmed, like this.

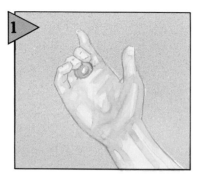

1

Pick up the grape from the table between the thumb and fingers of your right hand, so that the hidden grape is behind the visible one.

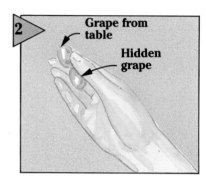

2

Grape from table

Hidden grape

3

Put the top grape into your mouth and leave the other one sticking out between your lips. It will look as if you have only one grape in your mouth.

4

When the audience has seen the grape between your lips, take it out with your right hand. Hold it between your first finger and thumb.

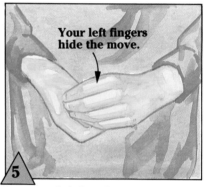

5

Your left fingers hide the move.

Put your left hand over your right as if to take the grape, but drop it onto your right fingers (a French Drop). Close your left hand as if it has the grape.

6

Drop you right hand casually into your lap and leave the grape there. At the same time, raise your left hand to the top of your head, watching it move.

7

Flatten your left hand and hit the top of your head. As you hit your head, spit out the grape from your mouth. Catch it in your right hand.

Tip

Remember not to say anything when you have a grape in your mouth which the audience is not supposed to know about.

Self-Raising Roll

This is a simple trick which is good fun. You need a fork, a bread roll and a napkin.

Practise in front of a mirror until it looks as if the roll is floating up of its own accord.

1 Secretly prepare the bread roll by sticking a fork into it at an angle, like this. Leave the roll and fork ready on the table, and lay a napkin over them.

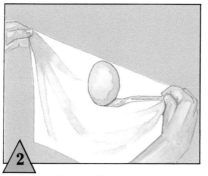

2 Hold the fork with your right thumb and first finger, and a corner of the napkin between your first two fingers. Holding the other corner with your left hand, lift the roll and napkin.

3 Lift the roll on the fork so that it can be seen above the napkin, but don't let the audience see the fork. Move the napkin up and down so that it looks as if the roll is floating.

Coin in Roll

Finding a coin in a bread roll is a good trick to do at the dinner table. Start with a coin Finger Palmed* in your right hand.

Pick up a roll in your left hand and shake it by your ear.  **1**

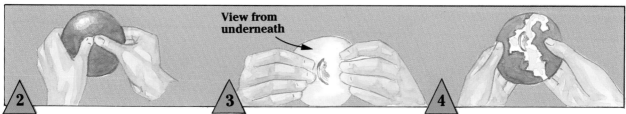

View from underneath

2 Hold the roll in both hands and press your thumbs down into the middle to break it open underneath.

3 Press up into the middle of the roll with your fingers, pushing the coin inside.

4 At the same time, break open the top with your thumbs to show the coin in the middle of the roll.

5 Look at the coin in surprise, pull it out of the roll, and slip it into your pocket.

Tip

Don't draw too much attention to the trick. People will still notice and they might even look for money in their rolls.

See p36 for how to Finger Palm a coin.

MORE PAPER TRICKS

Paper Fold

This is a simple way of making something small disappear. You need two identical pieces of paper about 9cm (3.5in) square. Follow steps 1-3 to make the prop. Then steps 4-7 tell you how to do the trick.

1 Fold both pieces of paper into thirds both ways, so that each piece is divided into nine equal squares.

Glue

2 Fold the paper into two packets with the middle squares as the backs. Stick them back to back.

Folded piece under here →

3 Unfold one piece to be ready to do the trick. Keep the other piece tightly folded underneath.

Passport to Heaven

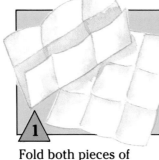

This is more an illustrated story than a trick, but it is entertaining. The speech bubbles tell you what to say and the text below the pictures tells you what to do.

There were two men trying to get to Heaven, one good and one bad.

1 Take a rectangular piece of paper and fold one of the top corners across to the opposite side of the paper.

When St. Peter asked for their passports, only the good man had one.

A   B

2 Now fold the other top corner down so that there is a triangle at the top of the sheet, like this.

Crosses Across

Crosses ← **Plain**

Left → ← **Right**

1 Before you start, take a piece of paper and draw four crosses on the left-hand half. Make sure the crosses cannot be seen through the paper.

2 Hold up the paper with the crosses facing you on the left. Tear it down the middle and turn the right-hand half around casually to show it is blank.

3 Put the right-hand piece in front of the left-hand piece, covering the crosses. Turn the pieces over and tear them both in half again.

4 Put the right-hand pieces in front of the left-hand ones and turn them over again. Tear them to make the pieces square. Put the right-hand half in front.

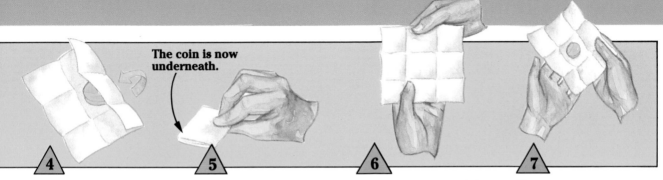

The coin is now underneath.

4

Borrow a coin or a ring from a member of the audience, and fold the top piece of paper around it.

5

Pick up the packet and turn it over causally, so the empty side in on top. Make a magic gesture over it.

6

Open up the top of the packet, keeping the other side hidden. The object you put inside has "vanished".

7

If you want to retrieve the object, fold the packet up. Turn it over again, and unfold it as before.

The bad man stole the passport and tore it up to stop the good man getting in.

Tear here

B

A

St. Peter took the pieces from the bad man, and saw he belonged to the devil.

But the bad man had dropped a piece, which the good man used as his passport.

3

Fold the paper in half so that A is on top of B, and tear two strips down through all the thicknesses.

4

Unfold the smaller pieces and put them together to make a devil shape. Leave the larger piece aside.

5

Pick up the larger piece of paper and unfold it, to show the audience that it is the shape of the cross.

Crosses

Volunteer

5

Turn the squares over and deal them in turn into two piles. The pile you deal to first will contain the crosses. Ask someone to choose a pile.

6

Whichever pile she picks, ask her to cover the one with crosses and give you the other.* Draw crosses on your pieces, then destroy them.

7

Ask her to show you her pieces. They have crosses on them. It looks as if the crosses have moved from your pieces of paper to hers by magic.

Tip

Always practise a trick with its patter, but don't forget when you perform that the story is new to your audience. If you sound bored, you will bore them, too.

Use Magician's Choice to do this – see p69.

103

COINS ON THE MOVE

Disappearing Coin

1 Hold a coin between your left fingers and thumb, and the corner of a handkerchief between the first and second fingers of your right hand.

2 Cover the coin with the handkerchief and drag it over the coin, moving your right hand towards you and keeping your left hand still.

Coin under here ↓

3 Do this again, but this time take the coin between your right thumb and first finger as you cover your left hand, still not moving this hand.

Through The Handkerchief

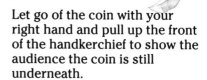

1 Hold a coin between your left forefinger and thumb. Cover the coin with a handkerchief.

2 Take hold of the coin through the handkerchief with your right hand. At the same time pinch a fold of cloth between your left thumb and the coin.

3 Let go of the coin with your right hand and pull up the front of the handkerchief to show the audience the coin is still underneath.

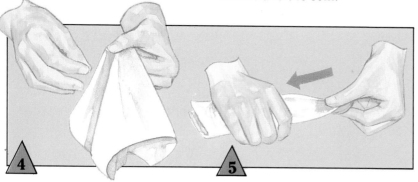

4 As you lower the front of the handkerchief again, flick your left hand so the side of the handkerchief nearest to you goes over to the front as well.

5 With your right hand, slowly pull the handkerchief, leaving the coin in your left hand. It appears to have gone straight through the cloth.

Tip

If your hands are tense and fidgety, try the actors' trick. Shake them hard before you start. It will help you relax.

Drop coin in top pocket.

4

When your right hand reaches your shirt front, you can drop the coin in your top pocket. Have something in the pocket to keep it open.

5

Slowly pull the handkerchief right over your hand and show that it is empty. Take the handkerchief in the other hand to show both hands are empty.

Tip

If you are not relaxed when you do a trick, it will make it harder for you to perform it well. Remember: the more you practise, the more relaxed you become.

Reappearing Coin

1

Lay a handkerchief over the palm of your left hand and pick up a coin in your right. Move your right hand towards your left, as if to place the coin in the handkerchief.

2

As you go to put the coin in your left hand, curl the fingers of your left hand to hide what you are doing.

3

Press the coin into your right fingers with your thumb, hiding it behind your fingers. Keep it Finger Palmed* as you move your right hand away.

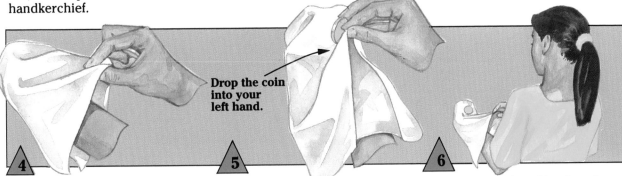

Drop the coin into your left hand.

4

Take the top corner of the handkerchief in your right hand and close your left. Pull the corner down to your left hand and back three times. Open your left hand. It is empty.

5

As you close your left hand, move your right hand forward again with the handkerchief. Drop the coin into your left hand and close your hand.

6

Pull your right hand back and tug at the handkerchief again. Then open your left hand and show the audience that the coin has reappeared.

See p36 for how to Finger Palm a coin.

105

TRICKS WITH GLASSES

Appearing Glass

This trick has built-in misdirection*. When you pretend to look for a coin in steps 2 and 5, you cover up for taking the glass and moving the handkerchief from one hand to the other.

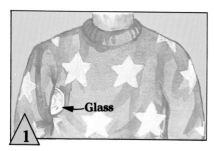

1

To prepare for the trick, secretly put a wine glass in your right armpit, with the base at the front. You could pull a little of your sleeve over the base to hide it.

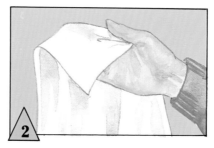

2

Show both sides of a handkerchief. Then drape it over your right hand, holding a corner between your thumb and palm. Hold it so it hides your right armpit.

3

Move your left hand behind the handkerchief, saying you are looking for a coin. Now take hold of the glass with the stem between your second and third fingers.

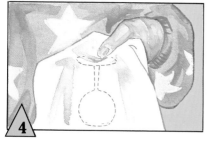

4

Move your left hand forward with the glass and take the handkerchief. Hold the top corner of the handkerchief between your thumb and the base of the glass.

5

Pretend to search your left side for a coin with your right hand. Then take hold of the top of the glass through the handkerchief and stand the glass up on your left palm.

6

Now pull the handkerchief off the top of the glass to reveal it standing on your hand. Polish the glass a little, then shake out the handkerchief and put it in your pocket.

Tip

Don't overact when you are trying to misdirect the audience or they will not be taken in.

Drink Bet

1

Place a full glass on a table. Say you will leave the room and the glass will be empty before you walk in again, although no-one else will touch it. Now walk out.

2

Crawl back into the room, reach onto the table and drink the contents of the glass. Crawl out of the room and then walk in again. You have won your bet.

* See p10-11 for misdirection.

Three Glass Trick

Put three glasses in a row on the table, with the middle one upright and the outside ones upside-down. The trick is to turn them all the right way up in three moves, turning two glasses each time. First demonstrate it to your volunteer like this.

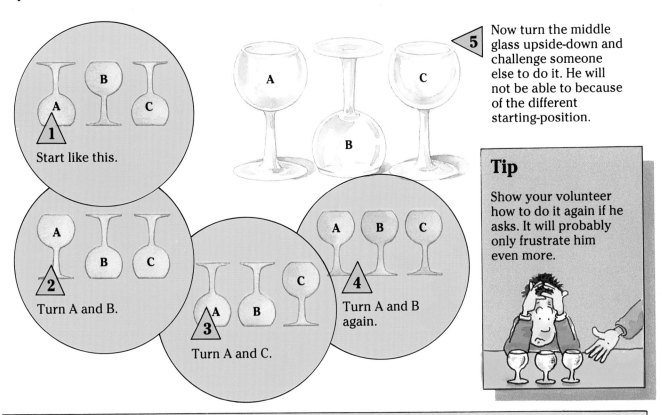

1 Start like this.

2 Turn A and B.

3 Turn A and C.

4 Turn A and B again.

5 Now turn the middle glass upside-down and challenge someone else to do it. He will not be able to because of the different starting-position.

Tip

Show your volunteer how to do it again if he asks. It will probably only frustrate him even more.

Six in a Row

If you have three empty glasses in a row with three full ones beside them, how can you move the glasses so that full and empty glasses alternate? You are allowed three moves, and each time you can only pick up two glasses, which must be next to each other.

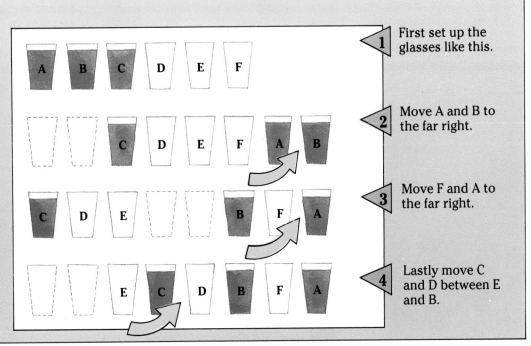

1 First set up the glasses like this.

2 Move A and B to the far right.

3 Move F and A to the far right.

4 Lastly move C and D between E and B.

Salty Knife

This trick uses the Paddle Move: this means that by twisting the knife in your hand, you show the same side twice, but the audience thinks it has seen both sides. Just before you start, secretly wet the blade of a table knife.

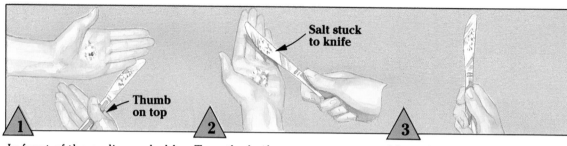

1 In front of the audience, hold the knife with the handle resting on your fingers, and your thumb on top. Pour some salt onto the blade.

Thumb on top

2 Turn the knife over, pretending to pour the salt into your other palm. Close your hand or the audience will see there is no salt in it.

Salt stuck to knife

3 Move the knife so it is upright in your hand with the salty side facing you. The audience must not suspect there is still salt on the knife.

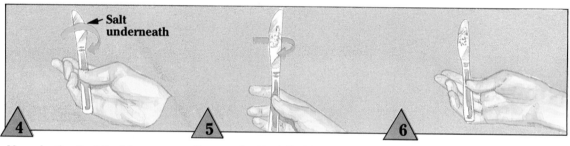

4 Now do the Paddle Move: lower the knife to its position in step 1, twisting it at the same time so the salty side is now facing the table.

Salt underneath

5 Repeat the Paddle Move to raise the knife so that it is vertical, twisting the knife back so the salty side is facing you again.

6 Now pretend to throw the salt in your other hand back at the knife, and lower the knife without twisting it to show the salt on the blade.

Tip

You could do these tricks to brighten up a meal. Everything you need is on the dinner table.

Sticky Fork

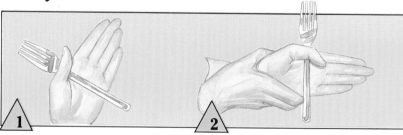

1 Lay your left hand palm-up on the table, and position a fork across your palm, like this. Hold it there with your left thumb.

2 Raise your hand with your palm towards you, holding the fork with your thumb, and your wrist with your right hand.

Spoon Bending

Acting is the key to this trick. If you look surprised at what you have done, the audience will think you have really bent the spoon.

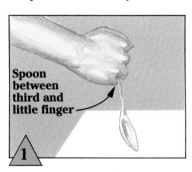

Spoon between third and little finger

1

Hold the handle of a spoon between the third and little fingers of your right hand, with your thumb on top.

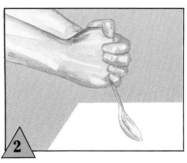

2

Curl your left hand over your right and hold the spoon upright, with the tip of the bowl resting on the table-top.

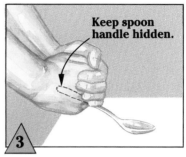

Keep spoon handle hidden.

3

Keeping your hands upright, suddenly bang them down onto the table. It looks as if you have bent the spoon.

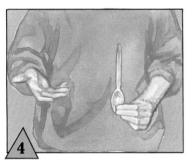

4

Pretend to be embarrassed for a moment. Then show the spoon and let everyone breathe a sigh of relief.

Tip

The only way to convince your audience that you are really bending the spoon is to pretend you are making some effort. If it looks too easy, no-one will be fooled.

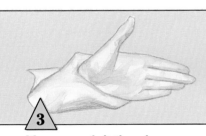

3

Move your left thumb away from your palm and watch the fork drop. Pretend to be disappointed and apologize to your audience.

4

Start again but this time as you raise your hand, extend your right first finger to hold the fork to your palm, unseen by the audience.

5

Slowly move your thumb away, leaving the fork "stuck" to your palm. After a while, drop the fork as if its power has worn off.

THE GLIDE

The Glide is a way of taking the next to bottom card from the pack but looking as if you are taking the bottom card. You may find this sleight difficult, but keep practising.

If you use new, smooth cards you may find it easier. When you can do the Glide without looking at your hands, try the tricks on these two pages.

1 ▷ Pick up the pack face-down with your thumb on one long side and your fingers on the other. Curl your second and third fingers far enough under the pack to get a grip on the bottom card. This is the Glide position.

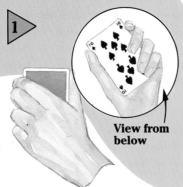

View from below

2 ▷ Now do the Glide: as you reach to take a card with your other hand, pull the bottom card back with your second and third fingers. Take the next to bottom card. Then slide the bottom card back into place with your fingers.

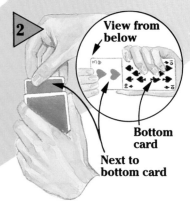

View from below

Bottom card

Next to bottom card

Red and Black

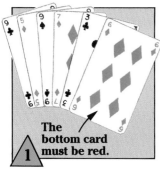

The bottom card must be red.

1 Arrange three red and three black cards of any suit and value in a fan, alternating the colours. Show them to the audience.

2 Holding the six cards in the Glide position, take the bottom card. Show it, saying "red", and put it on top of the others.

3 Now take the new bottom card, saying "black". Show it to the audience and put it on top of the cards, as you did the red one.

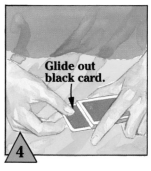

Glide out black card.

4 For the third card, Glide out the next to bottom card, saying "red". Put it on top of the cards without showing it.

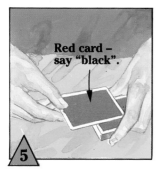

Red card – say "black".

5 Next take the bottom card again, and without showing it to the audience, say "black", and put it on top of the cards.

6 Take the new bottom card, saying "red", and show it to the audience before putting it on top of the other cards.

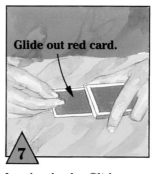

Glide out red card.

7 Lastly, do the Glide again and take the next to bottom card. Say "black", and put it on top of the cards without showing it.

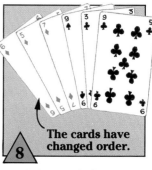

The cards have changed order.

8 Deal the cards face-down, saying "black, red, black, red, black, red". Snap your fingers and turn the cards face-up.

One in Three

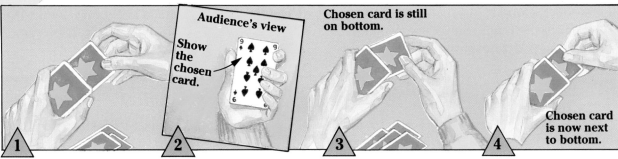

1 Shuffle the pack. Then hold it in the Glide position. Start dealing cards from the bottom of the pack, asking a volunteer to tell you when to stop.

2 When he does, show him the card on the bottom of the pack, without looking at it. Turn the pack down again and Glide out the next to bottom card.

Audience's view
Show the chosen card.

3 Tell the volunteer that you will now lose his card in the pack. Slide the card into the middle of the pack without showing it to him.

Chosen card is still on bottom.

4 Now Glide out another card, show it and say, "If you had stopped me one card later this would be your card." Put it on the bottom of the pack.

Chosen card is now next to bottom.

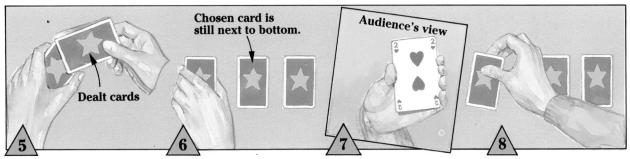

5 Show the top one of the dealt cards and say "If you had stopped me one card earlier this would be your card." Put the dealt cards on top of the pack.

Dealt cards

6 Put the pack face-down. Say you will cut the pack to find the chosen card. Cut off a third and put it to the right and another third to the left.

Chosen card is still next to bottom.

7 Pick up the left-hand pile in the Glide position and show the volunteer the card on the bottom, asking whether it is his chosen card.

Audience's view

8 When he says "No", turn the cards down again, then take this card off the bottom and put it face down. Lay this pile of cards to one side.

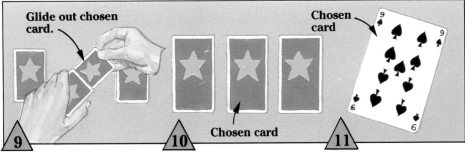

9 Next show the bottom card of the middle pile in the same way, but Glide out the next to bottom card. Put this card to the right of the first one.

Glide out chosen card.

10 Repeat steps 7 and 8 with the last pile, putting the bottom card to the right of the other two. Pretend to be disappointed at not finding the card.

Chosen card

11 Ask him to point to one of the cards. Us Magician's Choice* make sure he takes middle card, then a: him to show it. It is chosen card.

Chosen card

Tip

One in Three can be rather a long trick, so make sure your victim is a willing one before you start.

*For Magician's Choice see p69.

MENTALISM

Mentalist tricks are mind-reading effects or tricks where the magician seems to make things happen just by the power of thought.

These tricks are perhaps best performed with quiet confidence, although they can be very light-hearted.

Coincidence

This trick is a mentalist joke, which is good for a comical end to an act or a bit of fun with friends.

1 Ask someone to write any word on a piece of paper, saying you will read his mind and write exactly the same on your piece of paper. Encourage him to choose a word you will not know.

2 Pretend to concentrate hard on him as he writes his word.

3 Now write the words EXACTLY THE SAME on your piece of paper.

4 Ask him to reveal his word.

5 Announce triumphantly that you have accomplished the most difficult feat in mentalism: you have written exactly the same. Show what you have written to prove it.

Hypnotized Fingers

This is an effect which actually happens naturally, but which you appear to cause yourself.

Ask someone to clasp her hands tightly, extending her middle fingers, and hold them apart like this, keeping the others clasped.

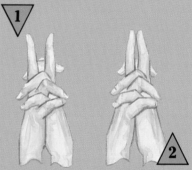

1

2

Move your hand towards hers, making a winding motion as if willing her fingers together. They will slowly move together.

Crazy Clock

1 To make the crazy clockface, cut a large circle of cardboard. Draw lines on one side to divide it into 12 equal sections. Write the numbers 1-12 in a jumbled order in the sections, and punch a hole in each section. Turn it over to prepare the other side.

2 Divide this side into 12 equal sections to match the ones on the other side. Write one letter of THE QUICK DOGS in each section, matching each letter to a number on the other side: T=12, H=11, E=10, Q=9, U=8, I=7, C=6, K=5, D=4, O=3, G=2, S=1.

Volunteer's number

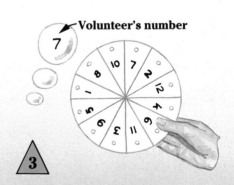

3 Ask a volunteer to pick a number on the crazy clockface. Say you will reveal his number by tapping the letters on the other side as he counts from 20 back to his number.

Find the Key

For this trick, you need a padlock with two keys which fit it, and three similar keys which do not. You need five identical envelopes and a bag to put them in.

To prepare for the trick, seal one of the keys which fit the lock in an envelope. Mark one corner on each side of the envelope with a pencil dot, and put it in the bag.

1

Ask four volunteers to check that only one of the four keys fits the lock. Ask them to mix the keys up and seal each one in an envelope. Put the envelopes in the bag.

2

Keep the marked envelope apart from the others.

3

Now take an envelope from the bag. Hold it to your head as if you are concentrating on it. You can see if it is marked. If if is not, lay it aside and take another envelope.

4

If you have taken four without finding the marked one, say you will start again. Push aside the envelope left in the bag so you can find it easily. Put the others back in the bag.

5

When you find the marked envelope, tear it open and give the key to the volunteer to try. It will open the lock. Casually tear up the envelope and throw it away.

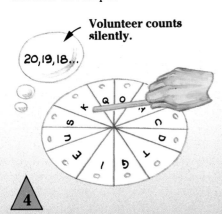

Volunteer counts silently.

20,19,18...

4

Turn the clockface over so only the letters show. Ask him to count silently, one number for each letter you tap. When he reaches his number, he must say "Stop".

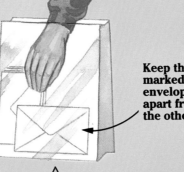

12...

5

Tap letters at random for the first eight taps, counting silently. For the ninth, tap the letter T, then tap letters in order, starting to spell out THE QUICK DOGS.

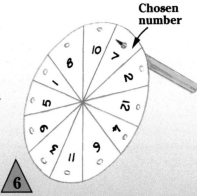

Chosen number

6

When he says "Stop", push the pencil through the hole in the section you are tapping. Show him the other side. The pencil goes through to his chosen number.

113

Vanishing Pencil

The pencil vanishes up your sleeve in this trick, so wear something long-sleeved. Start with a pencil in your right hand and a handkerchief draped over your left.

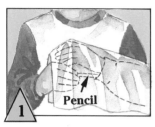

1 Move your right hand towards your left, taking the pencil under the handkerchief. As you do this, secretly push the pencil up your sleeve.

Pencil

2 Now extend your right forefinger and move your right hand away, covered by the handkerchief. It looks as if you are still holding the pencil.

Right forefinger extended

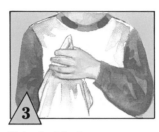

3 Take hold of your finger through the handkerchief with your left forefinger and thumb. Pull a couple of times and then give a sharp tug.

4 Pull the handkerchief off your right hand, bending your finger so you only reveal your empty hand. Shake the handkerchief. The pencil has vanished.

Fly Catcher

Steps 1-4 show you how to make a prop out of a piece of paper, and steps 5-8 suggest a way to use it. This is a trick which you can play on an unsuspecting friend.

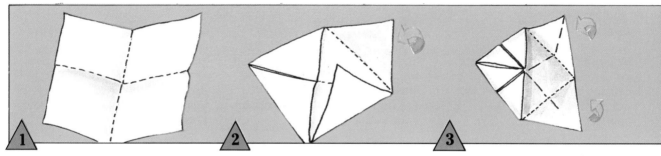

1 Take a piece of paper about 20cm (8in) square. Fold it in half both ways.

2 Next fold all the four corners into the centre.

3 Turn the paper over and fold the four corners into the centre.

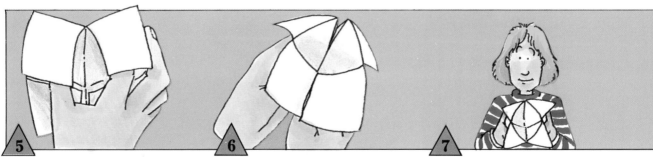

5 Now fit your your first fingers and thumbs into the pockets on the other side of the sheet.

6 Bring your fingers and thumbs together. By moving them differently you can show blank paper or flies.

7 Hold the catcher up to someone's mouth, showing the blank paper, and ask them to breathe into it.

Colour Pencil

Take a pencil out of your pocket, telling your friends it can write any colour they say. If someone says "red", twirl the pencil mysteriously. Then write RED on a piece of paper and give it to them.

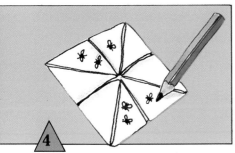

Draw some flies in four sections, like this.

As you take the catcher away, change it to show the flies to your victim, saying "Urggh".

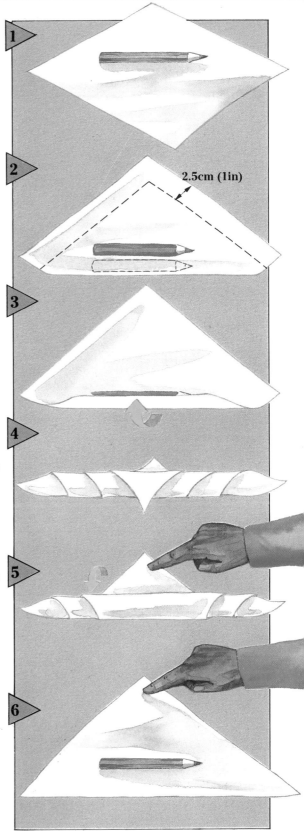

1 Lay a handkerchief flat on the table and place a pencil roughly in the middle of it, like this.

2 Fold the handkerchief diagonally, so that the top corner overlaps the one underneath by about 2.5cm (1in). Put a pencil of a different colour on top of the first one.

2.5cm (1in)

3 Roll up the handkerchief around both pencils.

4 Continue until you have rolled over one corner, so that the handkerchief looks like this.

5 Flick over the corner on the roll to cover the one still on the table. Hold it down.

6 Unroll the handkerchief, still holding this corner down. The pencils have swapped places.

Coin Through Hand

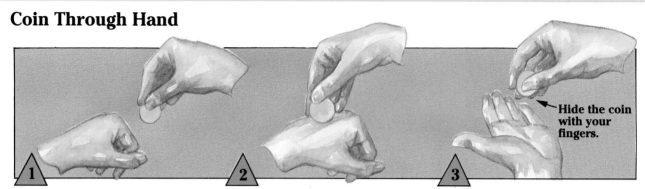

1 Hold a coin between the thumb and first three fingers of your right hand. Say you will push the coin through the back of your left hand into your fist.

2 Push the coin against the back of your hand, and let it slide up between your fingers and thumb. It looks as if the coin is going through your hand.

3 Turn your left hand over and open it, without moving your right hand. Say disappointedly **that the coin must be stuck halfway through.**

Hide the coin with your fingers.

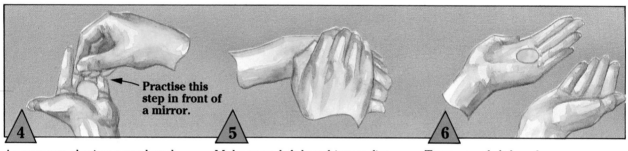

4 As you are closing your hand to try again, drop the coin from your right hand into your left. The fingers of your left hand will hide this move.

Practise this step in front of a mirror.

5 Make your left hand into a fist again. Now rub the back of your fist with the fingers of your right hand, as if you are pushing the coin through.

6 Turn your left hand over, saying you think the coin has arrived. Then open your fist to show that the coin is in the palm of your left hand.

Through the Table

Sit at a table with two coins near each other and close to the edge. Keep your legs together to catch a coin in your lap in step 4. For the trick to work best, keep the rhythm of the moves the same all the way through the trick.

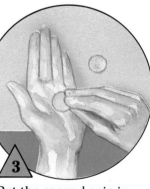

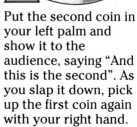

1 Pick up one of the coins with your right hand and put it in your left palm. Show it to the audience, saying "I need two coins to do this trick. This is the first one".

2 Turn your left hand over and slap the first coin on the table. At the same time, slide the second coin to the edge of the table with your right hand and pick it up.

3 Put the second coin in your left palm and show it to the audience, saying "And this is the second". As you slap it down, pick up the first coin again with your right hand.

Vanishing Coin

In this trick, you make a coin vanish into your trouser leg. Start by pressing the coin against the material of your trousers with your right thumb.

Pinch the material at the bottom of the coin with your right first finger. Fold it upwards to cover the coin, turning it over to rest against your thumb.

Hold the top of the fold in place with your left first finger, and take your right hand away, with the coin between your thumb and first three fingers.

Move your right hand, still holding the coin, below your left hand and tug the fold out of the material. The coin has vanished into your trouser leg.

Rubbing It In

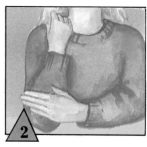

Bend your right arm to rest your hand against your neck, like this. Hold a coin in your left hand and say you will rub it through your sleeve.

Hold the coin in your left palm and rub it against your right elbow. Take your hand away. Pretend to be disappointed when the coin drops to the floor.

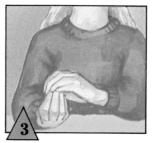

Coin

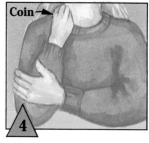

Pick up the coin in your right hand and say you will try again. Pretend to take the coin with your left hand, but French Drop it into your right.*

Bend your right arm and rub it again. At the same time drop the coin inside your collar. Take your left hand away. The coin has vanished.

Drop the coin into your lap.

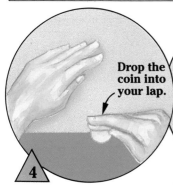

Put the first coin in your left hand and show it, saying "This is the first coin". Slap it down and slide the second coin to the edge of the table and drop it into your lap.

Imaginary coin

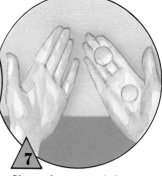

Lift your right hand as if it has a coin in it, and put this imaginary coin into your left hand. Close your left hand over it and say "And this is the second coin".

Imaginary coin under ← hand

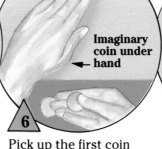

Pick up the first coin with your right hand and take it under the table. Now slap your left hand down and pretend to push the second coin through the table.

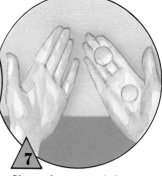

Show that your left hand is empty. At the same time, take the second coin from your lap with your right hand. Bring both coins above the table to show to the audience.

See p8 for the French Drop.

117

CARD FLOURISHES

A flourish in magic is something designed to catch the audience's attention. These pages explain how to do two flourishes with playing cards, and two tricks which use them. Try the tricks when you can do the flourishes really well.

The Riffle Shuffle

This flourish is an impressive way of shuffling cards which a lot of card players use. It is easier to do on a soft surface, so practise on a chair or carpet at first.

1 Divide the pack into two roughly equal halves. Square them up and place them face-down on the table, side by side.

2 Put your first fingers on top of the cards, with your other fingers on the outside long edges and your thumbs at the top inside corners.

3 Pushing the edges furthest from you down on the table with your fingers, lift the top inside corners of both halves with your thumbs.

4 Now move the two halves together, so the lifted corners overlap. Lift your thumbs slowly, letting cards drop off the bottom of both halves.

5 Carry on riffling the pack like this until all the cards have fallen, and the corners of the two halves of the pack are completely interlaced.

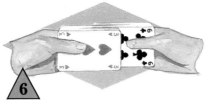

6 Now stand the cards on one long edge, interlacing the ends more. Push the halves into each other with your fingers until the pack is squared.

Riffle Location

Memorize this card.

1 Before you start, you need to set up the pack with all the clubs on top. They can be in any order. Memorize the top card.

Volunteer

2 Ask a volunteer to deal any number of cards between 1 and 12 face-down, and then to memorize the next card in the pack.

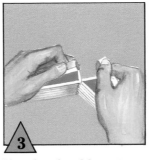

3 Next he should put it back, with the dealt cards on top of it. He should cut the pack and give it to you. Do two Riffle Shuffles.

Magician's card   Volunteer's card

4 Now look through the pack for the card you memorized. The volunteer's chosen card will be the club to the right of it.

The Charlier Cut

This flourish is a one-handed cut which takes some practice, but which looks very good once you have perfected it. Do it quite slowly so the audience can see.

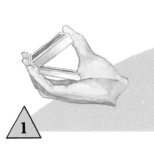

△1

Hold the cards by the long edges, face-down over your palm like this. Move your thumb slightly to let the bottom cards fall into your palm.

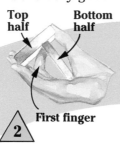

Top half   Bottom half

First finger

△2

Push the bottom half of the pack up and over the edge of the top half, using your first finger. Your other fingers should stay straight as you do this.

Top half   Bottom half

△3

As the bottom half comes up level with the top half, let go with your thumb, so that the top half drops into your hand under the bottom half.

△4

Move your first finger out from under the pack. Now square up the edges of the pack with your fingers and thumb, and the cut is complete.

Jumping Aces

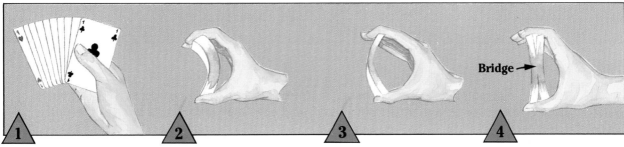

△1

To start the trick, openly put the ace of hearts on top of the pack and the ace of clubs at the bottom of the pack.

△2

Tell the audience that you are going to do something spectacular, and as you say it, bend the whole pack like this.

△3

Take off the top half of the pack and bend it the other way. Do this in a flourishy way to fit the character of the trick.

Bridge →

△4

You have now made a "bridge" in the pack. If you hold the cards gently when you cut them, they will cut at this place.

△5

Holding the pack ready to do the Charlier Cut, take the ace of clubs from the bottom of the pack. Name it and show it.

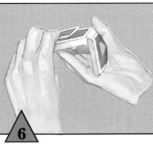

△6

Do the Charlier Cut up to step 3. Then put the ace of clubs in between the halves of the pack just before you complete the cut.

△7

Take the top card. Name it as the ace of hearts without showing it and put it into the pack while cutting, as in step 6.

△8

Spread the cards to show the aces have jumped back to their original positions at the top and bottom of the pack.

Quick Knot

This way of tying a simple knot works well with string or rope. It works so smoothly that the knot just seems to appear. You need a piece of string about 1m (1 yard) long.

Hold the string in your hands like this, with one end hanging behind your left hand and the other in front of your right palm.

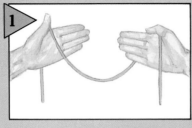

Now take hold of the string behind your left hand with your right fingers, and the string in front of your right hand with your left fingers.

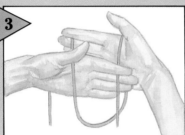

Bring your hands together so your right goes behind your left, parting the first and second fingers of each hand in a scissors action.

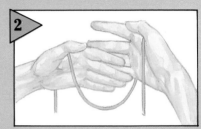

Pull your hands apart again, still holding the string between your fingers. A knot automatically appears in the string as your hands part.

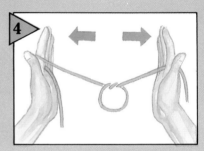

Free the Loop

In this trick, you make a loop escape from a piece of string. Don't say how many knots you are tying in step 3, or someone may check and see there is an extra knot at the end.

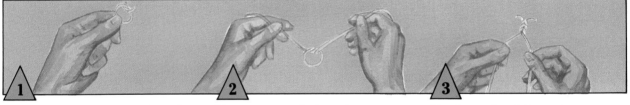

1 Before you start, make a loop by gluing a simple knot into a small piece of string. Put it in your back pocket.

2 Now tie a simple knot into a length of string. Pull it to make a loop the same size as the one in your pocket.

3 Tie the ends of the string together with several knots. Explain that they will keep the loop on the string.

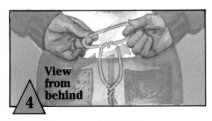

View from behind

4 Hold the string behind your back, saying you will remove the loop. Put your fingers into the loop.

View from behind

5 Still holding the string behind your back, pull the loop wider until it meets the knots at the ends of the string.

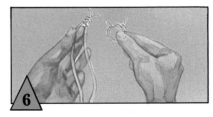

6 Secretly take the glued loop from your back pocket. Show it to the audience, separate from the string.

The Great Escape

This trick works best with two volunteers, as it is fun to watch. You can take part yourself if you have only one volunteer. You need two pieces of string about 1.5m (1.5 yards) long. The volunteers are called A and B to make it easier to follow the instructions.

1 Tie the ends of one piece of string to A's wrists, like this. Tie the knots carefully and make sure they cannot come undone by accident.

2 Now tie one end of the second string to B's left wrist. Pass it over and back under A's string. Then tie the other end to B's right wrist.

3 Give your friends five minutes to try to get apart without untying the strings. When they give up, tell them how to free themselves.

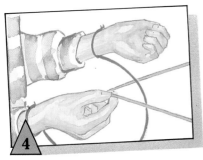

4 A must take hold of the string between B's wrists where it goes over his string, and pull it towards him. B may need to move closer to A.

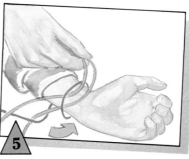

5 A now feeds the loop of B's string up through the string around his own left wrist, towards his hand. He must be careful not to twist it.

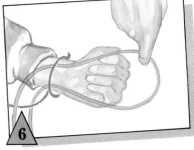

6 A pulls more string up to make the loop larger. Then he closes his left hand to make a fist small enough to pass through the loop.

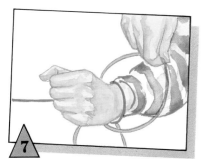

7 Now he passes the loop over his left fist and wriggles the loop over the back of his hand, still without twisting it.

8 A and B can slowly step apart. If they have done everything right, their strings will no longer be joined together.

Tip

You could do The Great Escape as an escapology stunt. Tie the second piece of string to two legs of a table and follow A's moves to escape.

JUMPING COINS

Coin Leap

This is quite a hard trick, although it can be done well with lots of practice. You need four identical coins for this trick.

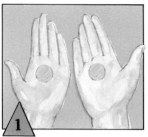

1 Place a coin in each of your palms. Close your hands, saying you will make a coin leap from one hand to the other.

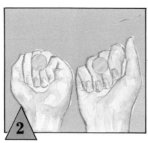

2 Ask a volunteer to put the other coins on your fingers. Shake your hands as if to make the coins jump.

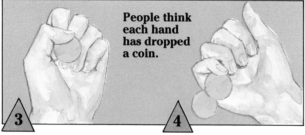

People think each hand has dropped a coin.

3 Quickly pull the coin on your left hand into your palm with your thumb. The shaking should help hide this move from the audience.

4 At the same time, shake the coin off your right hand and open your hand to let the coin in your right palm fall onto the table as well.

5 Apologize for having made a mistake and ask the volunteer to put the coins back on your hands. Then start shaking them as before.

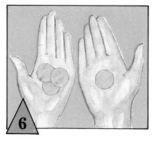

Volunteer

6 While you are shaking them, pull both coins into your palms with your thumbs. Open your hands to show one has "leapt" across to your left hand.

Tear the Coin

In this trick you fold up a coin in a piece of paper. You tear up the paper immediately, and the coin has vanished. You need a fairly large coin and a piece of paper 10cm (4in) square.

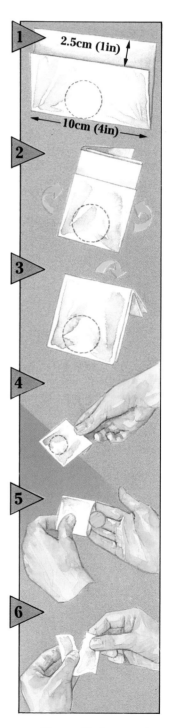

1 Fold the paper so that one side is about 2.5cm (1in) shorter than the other. Drop the coin into the fold.

2.5cm (1in)

10cm (4in)

2 Holding the paper with the shorter side towards you, fold the sides back behind the coin, like this.

3 Now fold the top 2.5cm (1in) behind the coin. You have made a pocket around the coin, with one end left open.

4 Take the pocket by the middle of the open end. Tap it on the table with your right hand to prove that the coin is still inside.

5 Take the pocket by the other end in your left hand, letting the coin slide out into your right hand. Finger Palm it.*

6 To finish, tear the paper into pieces and drop the bits. Put the coin in your pocket when no-one is looking.

* See p123 for how to Finger Palm a coin.

Hand to Hand

In this trick, you appear to transfer a coin twice from your right hand to your left by magic. You need five identical coins, four on the table and one Finger Palmed in your right hand. You need to keep a steady rhythm going when tossing the coins from hand to hand.

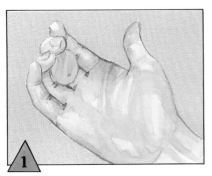

1

To Finger Palm a coin, rest it against the bottom joint of your middle two fingers. Bend them to hold it, leaving your other fingers relaxed.

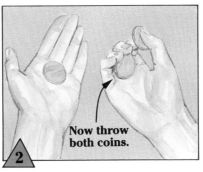

Now throw both coins.

2

Pick up a coin with your right hand and toss it across to your left. Repeat this, and this time throw the Finger Palmed coin as well.

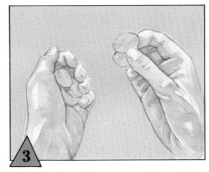

3

Pick up the other two coins with your right hand. Then close both of your hands and pause for a moment to make a grand magic gesture.

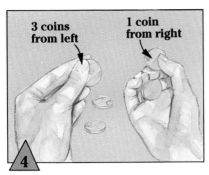

3 coins from left   1 coin from right

4

Drop the coins in your left hand on the table one by one. Also drop one coin from your right hand, keeping the other one Finger Palmed.

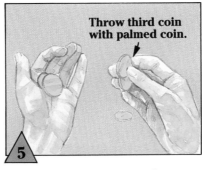

Throw third coin with palmed coin.

5

With your right hand, pick up and throw three coins to your left hand, one by one. Throw the Finger Palmed coin with the third one.

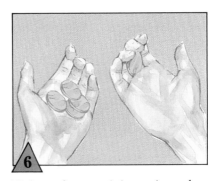

6

Pick up the remaining coin and leave it Finger Palmed in your right hand. Close your hands and make another magic gesture.

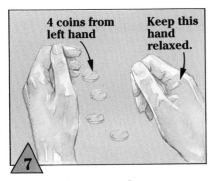

4 coins from left hand   Keep this hand relaxed.

7

Drop the four coins from your left hand one by one. Don't look at your right hand, and try to keep it relaxed, so it appears to be empty.

8

To finish the trick, casually pick up the four coins from the table in your right hand, one by one. Then put all five coins into your pocket.

Tip

When you have something hidden in your hand, don't make it obvious by holding your hand stiffly or by paying too much attention to it.

CARD SLEIGHTS

On these two pages you can learn how to do two sleights: the Backslip and the Palm.

Under the explanation of each sleight is a trick you can do using it.

The Backslip

This is one of the easiest card sleights, although it still takes practice. It is a way of cutting the cards to end up with the top card of the pack on top of the bottom half.

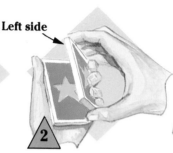

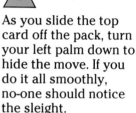

Left side

Grip top card.

1 Hold the pack face-down in your left palm, with your thumb against one long edge and your fingers curled around the other edge.

2 Take hold of the top half of the pack by the short edges with your right fingers and thumb. Lift the left side of the cards, like opening a book.

3 Now lift off the top half completely, gripping the top card with your fingers to pull it onto the bottom half of the pack. Do this quite quickly.

4 As you slide the top card off the pack, turn your left palm down to hide the move. If you do it all smoothly, no-one should notice the sleight.

Card Switch

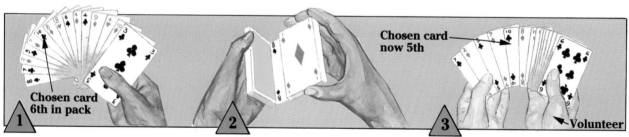

Chosen card 6th in pack

Chosen card now 5th

Volunteer

1 Ask someone to think of a number between 5 and 15. Show her the top 15 cards and ask her to memorize the one at her chosen number.

2 Now put the 15 cards back on top of the pack and cut the pack, doing a Backslip so that the top card goes onto the bottom half.

3 Give your volunteer the top half of the pack, keeping the bottom half yourself. Ask her to check quickly and confirm that her card is still there.

Volunteer

Volunteer's card is on your cards.

Volunteer thinks this is her card.

Chosen card

4 Now ask her to tell you the number she chose and count that many cards, less one, back onto your half of the pack.

5 Say you will pick a card by cutting your half of the pack, and do another Backslip at the same time.

6 Ask her to turn her top card over, and turn your top card. You have her chosen card on your half of the pack.

The Palm

Palming a card is hiding it in the palm of your hand. It takes a lot of practice, but will not be noticed when you can keep your hand relaxed with a card in it.

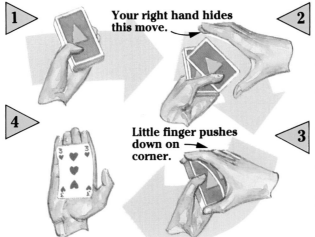

1 Hold the pack face-down in your left hand with your thumb on top and your fingers against one long side. Hold your thumb slightly bent.

Your right hand hides this move.

4 The bottom corner of the card should be wedged against the base of your thumb, like this. Hold the pack in your right hand for a moment, then pass it back to your left hand, keeping the card Palmed.

Little finger pushes down on corner.

2 Move your right hand to take the pack from your left. At the same time, straighten your left thumb, pushing the top card out at an angle to the others.

3 As you take the pack, push down on the top corner of the angled card with your right little finger and push it up with your left fingers. This levers it into your palm.

Pocket the Card

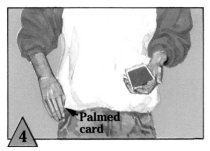

1 Ask someone to think of a number between 1 and 10. Show him the first 10 cards in the pack, counting them as you do so. Ask him to remember the card at his number.

Chosen card

2 Say you will try to find his card and put it in your pocket. Take a card more than ten down, but near the top of the pack. Look at this card, frown and put it on top of the pack.

3 Do this again, but this time, look at the card, smile and put it in your pocket. Now ask the spectator what number he thought of and deal him that number of cards face-down.

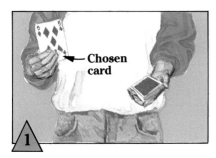

4 Ask the spectator to reveal his top card. At the same time, Palm the top card of the rest of the pack. Ask the spectator whether the card he has turned over is the one he chose.

Palmed card

5 When he says "No", reply "Of course not. I have it in my pocket". Reach into your pocket and produce the Palmed card, leaving the other one in your pocket.

Tip

You still have a card in your pocket at the end of this trick. Leave it for a while before taking it out, so people do not connect it with this trick.

MAGIC INFORMATION

Books

There are hundreds of books about magic and magic tricks. Look for them in your local library or a large bookshop. Here are some suggestions of books about specialized areas of magic. You should be able to get them from magic shops, or by mail order.

Introductory books

The Magic Book – Harry Lorayne
The Amateur Magician's Handbook – Henry Hay
Classic Secrets of Magic – Bruce Elliott

History of magic

The Illustrated History of Magic – Milbourne Christopher
The Great Illusionists – Edwin A. Dawes

Presentation and technique

Our Magic – N. Maskelyne and D. Devant
Magic and Showmanship – Henning Nelms
Forging Ahead in Magic – John Booth

Advanced and specialist books

The Royal Road to Card Magic and **Expert Card Technique** – Jean Hugard and Frederick Brauer
The New Modern Coin Magic – J. B. Bobo
It's Easier Than You Think – Geoffrey Buckingham (manipulation)
Anneman's Practical Mental Effects – Ted Anneman
Magic With Faucett Ross – Lewis Ganson (cabaret magic)
The Dai Vernon Book of Magic – Lewis Ganson (close-up and cabaret magic)
The Tarbell Course in Magic (7 volumes) – Harlan Tarbell

Magic conventions

At magic conventions, you can buy tricks, watch magic shows and meet other magicians. They usually last for one or two days. You can find out exact venues, dates and details in magic magazines.

Shops

For magic shops in your area, look in your local telephone directory. These are some well-known ones:

In Britain:

International Magic Studio,
89, Clerkenwell Road,
London EC1R

Tam Shepherds,
33, Queen Street,
Glasgow G1 3EF

In Australia:

Eric's Magic Den,
Myer,
Top of the Mall,
Brisbane

Bernard's Magic Shop,
211, Elizabeth Street,
Melbourne, VIC 3000

In Canada:

Perfect Magic,
4781, Van Horne Avenue
Suite 206, Montreal,
QUE. H3W 1J1

Morrissey Magic Ltd,
2882, Dufferin Street,
Toronto,
ONT. M6B 3S6

In the USA:

Louis Tannen Inc,
6, West 32nd Street,
New York, New York 10001

Abbott's Magic Company,
Colon, Michigan 49040

Mail order

You can get magic books and props by mail order from dealers who advertise in magazines, and from magic retailers.

This company deals in magic by mail order. Please note they only stock specialist books like the ones in the list on the left.

The Supreme Magic Company, Supreme House, Bideford, Devon EX39 2AN, England

Magic courses

Some professional magicians teach magic. If you are interested, although courses may be expensive, try looking in magic magazines for advertisements.

Magazines

You can subscribe to magic magazines or buy them in magic shops. Local clubs may also produce magazines.

In Britain:
Abracadabra,
Goodliffe Publications Ltd,
150, New Road, Bromsgrove,
Worcestershire B60 2LG

In Australia:
Australian Magic Monthly
Contact Tim Ellis (03-481-5832)

In Canada:
There are no Canadian magic magazines. Magic shops should stock British and American magazines.

In the USA:
Genii International Conjuror's Magazine, P.O. Box 3608, Los Angeles CA 90036

Magic societies

There are many magic clubs and societies: local, national and international. Inquire at magic shops to find ones in your area.

Unfortunately, many clubs have restrictions, such as that you must be over 18 or male to join. Two famous international societies are:

The Magic Circle

The Magic Circle is a club which only allows men over 18 to join, but anyone can seek information from them. If you would like to know more about it, write to this address:

The Honorary Secretary,
The Magic Circle,
c/o The Victory Services Club,
63/79 Seymour Street,
London W2 2HF, England

The International Brotherhood of Magicians

This is an international society with groups or "rings" in each country. It has its own magazine, "The Linking Ring".

In Britain:

IBM Secretary, King's Garn, Fritham Court, Fritham, Nr. Lyndhurst, Hampshire SP43 7HH

In Canada:

There are branches of the IBM in many big cities in Canada. Find them in your telephone directory.

In Australia:

Sydney Branch,
Kent Blackmore,
8/33 Muriel Street,
Hornsby, NSW 2077

ACT Branch,
Peter McMahon,
12, Clarkson Street,
Pearce, ACT 2607

In the USA:

IBM Executive Secretary,
P.O. Box 89,
Bluffton,
Ohio 45817

INDEX